Mills & Boon
Best Seller Romance

A chance to read and collect some of the best-loved novels from Mills & Boon—the world's largest publisher of romantic fiction.

Every month, six titles by favourite Mills & Boon authors will be re-published in the *Best Seller Romance* series.

A list of other titles in the *Best Seller Romance* series can be found at the end of this book.

Anne Mather

THE SMOULDERING FLAME

MILLS & BOON LIMITED
LONDON · TORONTO

First published 1976
Australian copyright 1982
Philippine copyright 1982
This edition 1982

© Anne Mather 1976

ISBN 0 263 74046 3

Set in 9½/11pt Plantin

02-1082

Made and printed in Great Britain by Richard Clay (The Chaucer Press) Ltd, Bungay, Suffolk

CHAPTER ONE

JUST standing still on the concrete platform, Joanna could feel rivulets of sweat running freely down her spine. The thin denim shirt and pants, worn to protect her from the blistering heat of the sun, clung revealingly to her slender figure, and she was not unaware of the many speculative stares from dark eyes cast in her direction. She had been in hot places before, but none so hot as this, and the insanity of trying to find a man she had not seen since she was four-teen years old was rapidly beginning to mean more to her than actually succeeding in her quest. Her father could have had no idea of the conditions here in Lushasa, or he would never have permitted her to come, she told herself. Or would he? Lately, his powers of reasoning had suffered quite a setback.

It had not seemed so insane in the peace and seclusion of the Lakeland fells where she had her home. The idea of a trip to Africa had sounded exciting, a chance of adventure which had unexpectedly come her way, possibly her last chance to do something on her own before settling down to marriage with Philip.

And finding Shannon had not seemed such an impossible pursuit. They had his address—or so they had thought, and the journey to Johannesburg had proved every bit as excit-ing as she had imagined. But someone else was living in Shannon's apartment in the high-rise block, and her visit to the government mining company there had proved fruitless. She had merely learned that five years before he had moved on to work for the Lushasan Mining Authority, and they had no forwarding address.

She had gone back to her hotel and cabled this news

5

home, half hoping that Philip, who had not been happy about her making the trip in the first place, would be able to persuade her father that she had done all she could. But she ought to have known that Maxwell Carne would not give up so easily. The answering cable had given instructions for her to travel to Menawi, the capital of Lushasa, and contact the mining authorities there.

Menawi, she had found to her surprise, was a fast-developing community, with well laid out shops and offices, modern hotels set in tropical gardens, and air-conditioning. Joanna's spirits had risen even more when, after checking into an hotel, she had telephoned the Lushasan Mining Authority and discovered that Shannon Carne was indeed employed by them. That he was working some two hundred miles distant at a place called Kwyana had not daunted her either, even though an elderly British couple staying at the hotel had warned her that conditions outside the capital were not half so civilised. She had been informed that there was an adequate train service running between Kwyana and the capital, built she assumed to accommodate the output from the mines, and she had looked forward to seeing something of the countryside.

It was not until she had emerged from the heat-laden atmosphere of the grimy carriage, hauled by a smoke-belching monster of an engine, and found herself on this desolate platform of concrete that she began to doubt the justification of her actions. Two hundred miles in distance meant a hundred years back in time so far as she could see. There was little evidence of the twentieth century here, with scrubland stretching towards purple shadowed mountains on one side of her, and close-set trees and creepers, noisy with the raucous cries of birds she could not begin to identify, encroaching almost to the iron tracks of the railroad on the other. The arrival of the train, and judging by the barriers this was as far as it went, was obviously quite an event. Dozens of Africans dressed in various garb

6

thronged the platform, hauling out crates of supplies and loading other crates aboard. Joanna was amazed that any-one knew which crates had to go where. The confusion was so immense, the noise so deafening, and always the heat to burn through to her prickling skin.

Beyond the peeling station buildings, a collection of shacks could be seen, and Joanna realised that she could not stand here indefinitely. She wondered uneasily how long the train would remain at the station, and whether, if by some terrible coincidence she missed Shannon, she could get back to Menawi that night. She had brought only an overnight case with her, leaving most of her belongings at the hotel.

Near the station barrier, the lorry which was supplying the crates being loaded on to the train bore the lettering: LUSHASAN GOLD MINING AUTHORITY, and her drooping spirits lifted a little. Picking up her case, she endeavoured to thrust her way between the Africans who were causing such an uproar, brushing against gleaming black bodies, aromatic with sweat, striped tent-like garments, denims and ordinary European gear.

The man in charge of the off-loading was not African, but neither was he wholly European. Joanna guessed he was a mixture of both, with handsome olive-skinned features and curly dark hair. His dark eyes widened to an incredible degree when he saw a white girl pushing her way towards him, and he spat commands at the Africans still blocking her path so that she could reach him without further effort. In a mud-coloured bush shirt and shorts, his sleeves circled with sweat, he nevertheless represented sanity in a world gone mad.

'*Mademoiselle!*' he exclaimed, giving her a perfunctory bow. '*Qu'est-ce que vous voulez? Ce n'est pas——*'

'Oh, please,' Joanna broke in, 'do you speak any English?' Her French, remembered from schooldays, was not very good, and she prayed that this man had some knowledge of

7

her own language.

'Yes, *mademoiselle*, I speak English.' The man gestured to the gaping Africans to get on with the unloading. 'But what is an English young lady doing here?' He spread his hands expressively. 'You cannot be travelling alone?'

His accent was attractive, but Joanna was in no mood to appreciate it. 'I am travelling alone, yes——' she was beginning, only to be interrupted by a flow of invective from his lips as one of the Africans dropped a crate right behind them. After a moment, her companion turned back to her and apologised, indicating that she should go on.

Joanna tried to gather her thoughts, but this was all so strange to her, not least the way this man could switch from smiling urbanity to obviously crude abuse in seconds.

Forcing herself to ignore their faintly hostile audience, she said: 'Could you direct me to the mine, please?'

'The mine, *mademoiselle*?'

'You are from the gold mine, aren't you?' Joanna made an involuntary movement towards the lettering on the cab of the lorry.

He looked in that direction himself, and then swung his head curiously back to her. 'You want to go to the mine, *mademoiselle*?'

Joanna tried not to feel impatient. 'Obviously.'

He shrugged, tipping his head to one side. 'The mine is over there, *mademoiselle*.' He indicated the distant mountains.

Joanna stared in dismay towards the purple-shrouded range. 'But that must be—five or ten miles away!'

'Seven, to be exact,' her companion informed her, thrusting his hands into the hip pockets of his shorts.

'*Seven miles*!' Joanna's echo of his words was anguished.

'Why do you wish to go to the mine, *mademoiselle*?' the man asked softly.

Discarding prevarication, Joanna sighed. 'I've come to find my brother. I believe he works for the mining company.

8

Shannon Carne?'

The man beside her looked surprised. 'Mr Carne is your brother?'

'My half-brother, yes.'

'Half-brother?' He frowned. 'What is this?'

Joanna felt like telling him it was none of his business, but so far as she knew he might present her only chance of reaching the mine.

'It means we had the same father—different mothers,' she explained shortly. 'He is there, then? You do know him?'

'Yes, *mademoiselle*.' The man bowed his head. 'I know Mr Carne. But——' His eyes flickered over her for a moment. 'I did not know he had a—sister.'

There was something offensive in his appraisal, and Joanna felt her flesh crawl. But short of alienating the only person who might offer her a lift to the mine, there was nothing she could do. Perhaps he thought she was only masquerading as Shannon's sister. Perhaps wives or girl-friends were not allowed at the mine, and he thought she was only pretending a relationship. It was her own fault. She should not have come here so precipitately. She should have cabled ahead that she was in Lushasa, waited at the hotel in Menawi, trusted that after having come so far, Shannon would at least have the decency to come and see her.

If only he had replied to her father's letters, but of course, they had gone to Johannesburg, and he had left no forwarding address. He could have advised them that he had left South Africa. That awful row between him and his father had been all of ten years ago now. Had he never wondered about them in all that time? Never cared to know how they were? Little wonder if this man had doubts about their relationship. Since coming to Africa, Shannon had had no contact with his family whatsoever.

That was why Joanna had impulsively boarded the train and come to Kwyana. She could not have borne for

Shannon to ignore her, and by coming here she had eliminated any excuses he might make. Besides, she was eager to see him again. He had always been her hero, someone she had looked up to and admired. He had appeared to accept the fact of his parents' divorce when he was six years old without question, and when his father had married again and subsequently produced Joanna, he had shown no jealousy. Eight years her senior, he had taught her to swim and play games as well as any boy of her age, and she had idolised him. He had never talked about his mother or her rejection of him, even though they had known she was alive and well and living in America at that time, and that was why Joanna had found his rejection of the family so hard to take when it happened. She only knew that the row he had had with his father had something to do with his mother, and he had walked out of the house and never come back. For a while her father had been terribly bitter about the whole thing, but later on he had employed a private detective to find him. The man had traced Shannon to Witwatersrand, but although they had written, he had never replied to any of their letters. And now her father was sick, slowly dying in fact, and in spite of everything insistent that Shannon should inherit the estate.

Now Joanna squared her shoulders, and said: 'Well, I can assure you, I am Joanna Carne. And I do need to see my brother.'

The man considered her for a few moments longer, and then he said: 'Does—Mr Carne expect you?'

Joanna sighed. 'No.' She paused. 'He doesn't even know I'm in Africa. Does it matter?' She controlled a momentary irritation. 'Is there any vehicle I can hire to get to the mine?'

'There are no taxis here, *mademoiselle*.' The man's lips twisted derisively. 'But . . .' His appraisal abruptly ceased as he slapped at an insect crawling across his cheek. 'Perhaps I could take you there myself.'

Joanna expelled her breath with some relief. 'Oh, would

you? I'd be very grateful, Mr—er—Mr——'

'Just call me Lorenz,' replied the man, turning away to shout more abuse at the flagging porters. Then: 'Is this all your luggage?'

'Yes.' Joanna felt obliged to explain: 'I left the rest at the hotel in Menawi.'

'You did?' The man called Lorenz raised dark eyebrows. 'Then let us hope it is still there when you get back, eh?'

This was one worry Joanna refused to consider. 'I'm sure it will be,' she said equably, and allowed him to take her overnight case from her sticky fingers.

Her handbag swinging from her shoulder, Joanna stood waiting nervously for the unloading and loading to be through. The sun was burning the top of her head, and although she had piled up the honey blonde hair for coolness, damp strands were tumbling about her ears. She hoped her hair would be thick enough to withstand the heat of the sun, but she somehow doubted it. She felt as though every inch of clothing was sticking to her, and she thought longingly of pools of cool water, or the stinging spray of the shower back in the hotel. The water there had not been really cold, but it had been refreshing, and she longed to feel her skin tingling with cleanliness again after that interminable train journey. She was hot and grubby, and only the knowledge that Shannon was only seven miles away stopped her from climbing back aboard the train to Menawi.

'Perhaps you would prefer to wait in the cabin, Miss Carne?'

Lorenz was back, indicating the driving cabin of the lorry, and after a moment's hesitation Joanna nodded her thanks. She was glad she was wearing trousers as he helped her up. There was nothing ladylike about scrambling up iron footholds on to a seat that scorched like a hot tin roof. But she managed to smile down at her rescuer, and after a few moments of discomfort she could relax.

Flies buzzed in and out of the open doors, the noise outside had not abated, and her mouth felt dry and sandy. She had had nothing to eat or drink since breakfast in the hotel that morning, and as it was now afternoon, she was beginning to feel decidedly empty. An opened can of beer rested on the floor of the cabin, but the flies invading the twist-off lid made her feel sick.

After what seemed like hours, but which was in reality only about twenty minutes, Lorenz appeared below her. 'Almost finished now, Miss Carne. Soon we will be on our way.'

Joanna forced a smile. 'Oh, good.' She shifted a little under that irritating scrutiny. 'Will it take long? To get to the mine, I mean?'

Lorenz shrugged. 'Twenty-five—thirty minutes, no more.'

'So long?' Joanna couldn't prevent the exclamation.

Lorenz's expression hardened. 'Is not a good road, Miss Carne. You want I should break an axle?'

'Oh, no, of course not.' Joanna was quick to apologise. 'You must forgive me. I—I've never been in Africa before.'

Lorenz shrugged and turned away, and Joanna looked frustratedly down at her hands. She didn't want to antagonise the man, but thirty minutes to do seven miles seemed an exaggeratedly long time. She half wished there was some other way she could get there. She didn't like Lorenz's attitude towards her. She was convinced he did not believe that she was related to Shannon, and in his eyes, if she was not, what did that make her?

At last, a creaking and a heavy thud heralded the end of the delay. The lorry was loaded up, and Lorenz came to swing himself behind the wheel of the vehicle. The rank smell of sweat from his body as he levered himself into the cabin beside her made Joanna hold her breath for a moment, and his language when he accidentally kicked over the can of beer and sent a stream of brown liquid across his canvas-clad feet shocked and revolted her.

12

The engine of the vehicle started without trouble, and soon they were bumping over the siding, passing the shacks where groups of women watched them curiously, sounding the horn as almost naked children ran carelessly in their path. Then even those few signs of habitation were left behind, and they rolled heavily along a road split by the constant rays of the sun.

Joanna soon appreciated the wisdom of not travelling at speed. The lorry was built for carrying anything but passengers, and the end of her spine was soon numb from the buffeting it was receiving. From the somewhat sardonic glances Lorenz kept making in her direction, she guessed he knew exactly how she was feeling, and she determinedly put a brave face on it.

The sight of a herd of zebra some distance away across the plain brought a gasp of delight to her lips, and for a while she was diverted from her thoughts. Coming up from Menawi, she had seen little of the game for which West Africa was famous, and now she turned to Lorenz and asked him whether there were elephants and lions in this part of the country.

'There is a national safari park, Miss Carne. You can see plenty of game there. Here—well, occasionally I have seen a family of lions, and once we had a rogue elephant causing trouble at the mine, but man brings death to the animals, so they stay away.'

Joanna shook her head. 'That's awful, isn't it?'

'Wealth, too, has its price, Miss Carne. Once the game was the gold of Africa, but no more.'

'Are you—were you born in Lushasa, Mr—er—Lorenz?'

He looked her way. 'No. I was born in the Cape, Miss Carne. That is, South Africa. But I found the—climate here more to my liking.'

Joanna acknowledged this, and for a while there was silence. Then, without preamble, he said: 'How long is it since you have seen your—er—brother, Miss Carne?'

Joanna straightened her back. 'Some time,' she replied evasively. 'Do you—do you know him well?'

'A man in my position does not know the General Manager of the Kwyana Mine very well,' replied Lorenz bitterly.

'General Manager!' Joanna's involuntary ejaculation could not be denied. She had known her brother had taken a degree in engineering. Her father had been furious about it at the time, maintaining that an agricultural college would have served him better than a university. But obviously Shannon had put his knowledge to good use.

Lorenz was raising his eyebrows. 'You did not know your brother was so important?'

'No.' Joanna made an impatient little gesture. 'I've told you, it's some time since—since I saw him.'

'What a pleasant surprise, then. A man in Carne's position should be worth some small investment, wouldn't you say?'

Joanna caught her breath. 'I don't know what you're implying, Mr Lorenz, but I can assure you that my sole purpose here is to deliver a message to him from our father!'

Lorenz studied her flushed face for a moment, and then shrugged, returning his attention to the road. 'You may not find that so easy right now,' he commented cryptically.

'What do you mean?' Joanna stared at him.

His fingers flexed against the wheel. 'Our gallant Manager is ill, Miss Carne. I would doubt your ability to deliver any message to him during the next forty-eight hours.'

'*Ill*?' Joanna felt cold inside. 'What is it? What's wrong with him?' She put a hand to her throat. 'There—there hasn't been an accident——'

'Oh, no, no.' Lorenz shook his head, his tone mocking. 'Nothing so exciting, I assure you.'

'Then what is wrong with him?' Joanna couldn't hide her anxiety, or her impatience.

'Just a touch of fever, Miss Carne.' Lorenz was irrita-

14

tingly indifferent as he drawled the words. 'Just a little fever.'

'Fever!' Joanna shifted restlessly. 'What kind of fever?'

'Relax, Miss Carne. Your concern does you credit, but it is nothing to get excited about. In a couple of days your —er—brother will be as good as new, no doubt.'

Joanna's brows were drawn tight together above worried eyes. 'You should have told me sooner,' she exclaimed.

'Why?' Lorenz swung the lorry to avoid an enormous cavity yawning in the road, and she had to clutch the seat to prevent herself from being thrown against him. 'We could have got here no sooner. Unless—unless in his—er—debilitated state you might have decided not to come.'

Joanna did not answer this. She was too tense to exchange abuse with this man who seemed to be enjoying imparting such information, and besides, she didn't really know whether he was telling her the truth. But if he was, then perhaps it might have been better if she had not come ...

The mountains were nearer now, and as they began to climb the steeper gradient, the air became blessedly cooler. She guessed it was the breeze coming through the open windows of the vehicle which created the coolness and that outside it was still enervatingly hot, but any respite was a relief.

'Not much farther now, Miss Carne,' remarked Lorenz, as their wheels churned up a cloud of fine grey dust, and it was questionable whether the dusty air coming through the windows was preferable to closing them and suffering the heat inside. 'Just beyond this bluff—see!'

Opening out below them was a rugged valley, its base a startling mass of machinery and buildings. After so much that was primitive, the Kwyana mine was aggressively modern, and Joanna was astonished at its size and industry. As well as the buildings immediately adjacent to the mine workings, there was living accommodation for over three

15

hundred men, Lorenz volunteered, pointing out laboratories, ventilation and processing plants, the pumping station and mine hospital, as well as the enormous plant which powered the whole complex.

'Impressive, is it not?' Lorenz commented dryly. 'Over three hundred men, and not a woman—a white woman, at least, within a hundred miles. Except yourself, Miss Carne.'

Joanna did not answer this, but her nerves tightened at his words. If that were so, she ought not to have come here, and she had the feeling that Shannon would not appreciate her having done so. If only they had told her in Menawi how remote the mine was! But then she had not told them that she intended making the journey here herself.

At this hour of the afternoon there were few men about, but those there were stared with unconcealed amazement at Lorenz's companion in the cab of the lorry. Joanna could feel the hot colour in her cheeks adding to the general discomfort of her body, and she did not like the amusement Lorenz made no effort to hide.

The layout of the site reminded her of an industrial estate back home, only here two-storied dwellings mingled with steel-ribbed girders and the intricate maze of a chemical processing plant. Had it not been for the heat which, even though the sun was slowly losing its power, was still intense here in the valley, they could have been in any industrial complex anywhere in the world.

Looking about her, Joanna finally had to ask: 'Which of these blocks does my brother occupy?'

'None of them,' replied Lorenz laconically, startling her for a minute until he added: 'Managers don't live in blocks. They have houses. It's not much further. Have patience, Miss Carne.'

The sarcasm was back and Joanna clenched her lips. They had turned off the main thoroughfare on to a narrow track leading between the living blocks which were interspersed here and there with stretches of scorched grass.

Occasionally she caught glimpses of men playing football behind the buildings, but mostly her attention was fixed on the corrugated-roofed bungalows she could see ahead of them. There were several, set at intervals between scrub hedges, all alike with stuccoed walls painted in pastel shades, and overhanging eaves. Lorenz brought the heavy vehicle to a halt before one of them. The place looked deserted, the blinds were drawn and there was no apparent sign of life.

'That's it,' he announced derisively. 'I hope you don't find it disappointing.'

Joanna was sure he hoped she did, but she thrust open her door and climbed down quickly before he could offer his assistance. He handed her out her suitcase, and she had perforce to thank him.

'I don't know how I'd have managed without you,' she admitted.

'Nor do I,' he agreed, and let out his clutch; the lorry trundled noisily away.

After he had gone, it seemed incredibly quiet. The tiring journey on the train, the uproar at the station, and the trip in the lorry had all taken their toll of her nerves, and even the low throbbing sound which was all she could hear was welcome. Even so, she half thought her arrival would have disturbed someone, but no one appeared to have noticed.

Stifling the awful feeling of panic which was welling up inside her, Joanna picked up her suitcase and walked determinedly up the path to a meshed door. An outer door stood wide, but the meshed door had a self-closing hinge.

Feeling rather like an interloper, she knocked at the wood which surrounded the mesh and mentally composed how she was going to introduce herself. What if Shannon didn't recognise her? She was sure she would recognise him. His image was printed indelibly on her mind.

No one answered her knock, and with a sigh she knocked

harder. Still there was no response, and she shaded her eyes with one hand and looked hopefully up and down the road. What if Lorenz had brought her to the wrong bungalow? He might have done so deliberately. If only there was someone she could ask.

But the empty road mocked her, and the drawn blinds on the adjoining bungalows did not encourage intruders. When no one replied to her third attempt to attract attention, she tentatively opened the meshed door and went in.

She found herself in a narrow hall covered by some rubber flooring, but otherwise bare. The hall appeared to run from front to back of the building, with several doors opening from it. On impulse, Joanna opened one of these doors and peeped into the room beyond. She saw what appeared to be a study with a desk strewn with papers, a chair, a filing cabinet, and two telephones. A second door revealed a living room—armchairs, dining chairs and table, bookshelves, and a drinks cabinet.

Joanna closed this second door and stood, undecided. If this was not Shannon's house she was taking dreadful liberties, and even if it was, she had no way of knowing what his reaction to her presence there might be. Perhaps she should go outside again and wait until someone did appear. Surely—she consulted the slim masculine watch on her wrist—surely the day's work must almost be over. The men who lived in the other bungalows might be returning to them.

She was moving away towards the door when a low groan reached her ears. Immediately she stiffened, her heart pounding rapidly in her chest. The sound was coming from a room further along the hall, and with comprehension came the realisation that Lorenz had not been lying when he had told her that Shannon was ill.

Putting down her case again, she went stealthily along the hall and pressed her ear to the panels of the door. There was no further sound from within, but her hand had found the

18

handle and she could not resist turning it.

The room beyond was darkened, but blessedly cool. Whatever else these bungalows lacked, they had air-conditioning, and for a moment it was heaven for Joanna to feel the cool air against her over-heated skin. But then her eyes adjusted themselves to the dimness and she could make out the figure of a man tossing and turning on a narrow bed. Her nails digging into her palms, she moved forward, and then drew back again as she realised the man was naked. He had kicked the thin cotton sheet aside, and although his body was streamed with sweat, she could see he was shivering.

Joanna hesitated only a moment longer, and then moved forward once more, gathering the sheet from the foot of the bed and drawing it up over his shuddering limbs. Mosquito netting hung suspended over the bed, but when she brushed it aside she could see his face, and a curious weakness assailed her. Shannon's eyes were glazed and unseeing, but they were the same tawny eyes she remembered, the same heavy lids and long curling lashes. He had changed a little; after all, he was ten years older and therefore more mature. Nevertheless, the lean intelligent features were not so different, and from what she had seen of his muscled body, he still hadn't an ounce of spare flesh on him. His dark brown hair was longer than it had been, but it was just as thick and virile, and her fingers trembled as she touched it now, smoothing a heavy swathe back from his damp forehead. Her fingers lingered against his burning skin, needing that physical contact, but as he fought her attempts to keep the sheet over him, she looked round desperately, wondering what she could do. She felt angry as she wondered how long he had been lying here like this without anyone to care for him. Why wasn't he in the hospital Lorenz had shown her receiving proper attention?

'Shannon,' she ventured at last, sitting down on the side of the bed. 'Shannon—it's me, Joanna! Do you remember

19

me?'

Her softly spoken words seemed to penetrate his delirium, and for a few seconds there was a look of faint recognition in the eyes he turned in her direction. But then it disappeared, and he began twisting restlessly again, licking his lips as if he was parched.

'Who are you? What do you think you're doing?'

The cold angry words brought Joanna almost guiltily to her feet and she turned to find a woman entering the room. In a white uniform, she was probably a nurse, Joanna decided, and she made an involuntary gesture of apology.

'I—I'm Joanna Carne,' she explained awkwardly. 'Shannon's—sister.'

The woman's dark brows drew together uncomprehendingly, and as she drew nearer Joanna could see that like the man Lorenz, she was of mixed blood. But the combination was quite startlingly beautiful. Smooth olive features, lustrous dark eyes, and a wide sensuous mouth, her dark hair confined with madonna-like severity at the nape of her neck, she was unlike any nurse Joanna had ever seen, and her presence in this room emphasised the gulf which had opened between Shannon and his family more surely than the distance of miles could have done.

'*You*—are Shannon's sister?' The woman shook her head now. Then: 'What are you doing here—Miss Carne? Your brother is ill, as you can see. Please wait outside and I will speak with you after I have attended to my patient.'

The way she said those words made them an order, not a request, and the curtness of her tone caught Joanna on the raw. She had travelled thousands of miles to find her brother, and he was *her* brother, after all. How dared this woman, this stranger, nurse or otherwise, order her out of his bedroom?

'There was no one about when I arrived,' she stated, annoyed to hear the defensive note in her voice. 'I let myself in, and when I heard—groaning, I came to see if there was anything I could do.'

'Well, there is not.' The nurse's eyes were coolly appraising as she held up her hand to reveal the syringe she was holding. 'As I have already suggested, if you will wait outside . . .'

'What is that?' Joanna looked anxious.

The nurse sighed, displaying the tolerance she might have shown to a child. 'It is quinine, Miss Carne. Nothing more alarming than that. Now, if you don't mind . . .'

Joanna almost protested, but one look at Shannon still tossing on the bed silenced her. Arguing with this woman was only delaying his treatment, and she had the feeling she would be wasting her time anyway. With a shrug of her shoulders, she walked towards the door, and as she reached it she looked back and saw the woman drawing down the sheet and taking Shannon's right arm between her fingers. Joanna watched for a moment longer, and then, as the woman turned impatient eyes in her direction, she pressed her lips together and left the room.

CHAPTER TWO

JOANNA paced up and down the living room, her cork-soled sandals squeaking on the rubber-tiled floor. But she was too disturbed to sit and wait patiently for the nurse to come and speak to her, and with every minute that passed she grew more and more frustrated. How much longer was she to be kept waiting? What was going on in Shannon's bedroom? Surely it didn't take this long to give someone an injection.

There was the sound of footsteps behind her, and she swung round in relief, only to find a black youth in white shirt and shorts staring at her from the open doorway. He looked as surprised to see her as she was to see him, but like the nurse he obviously considered he had the prior authority here.

'You waiting to see Mr Carne, missus?' he asked frowning. 'You can't. He sick. He not seeing anyone.'

Joanna sighed. 'I know he's sick, but I have seen him.' Then as his dark eyes mirrored his alarm, she hastened on: 'I'm Mr Carne's sister. From England.' She waited until this was absorbed, and then added a question of her own. 'Who are you?'

The youth looked taken aback. 'Jacob, missus,' he answered reluctantly, glancing over his shoulder. 'You seen Miss Camilla?'

'Miss Camilla?' Joanna folded her arms, supporting her chin with the knuckles of one hand. 'Would that be—the nurse?'

Jacob nodded. 'Miss Camilla looking after Mr Carne.'

Joanna inclined her head. 'Yes, I've seen her.' She paused in front of him. 'Do you work for Mr Carne?'

Jacob shifted under her scrutiny. 'I Mr Carne's house-boy,' he admitted, his chin jutting proudly. 'Jacob best houseboy in Kwyana.'

'I'm sure you are,' agreed Joanna dryly. 'Tell me, how long has Mr Carne been ill?'

'Two days, Miss Carne.' The nurse's cool tones overrode Jacob's reply. 'I told you I would answer your questions as soon as I had attended to my patient.' She looked at the houseboy. 'That's all right, Jacob, I can handle this. You can go.'

'Yes'm, Miss Camilla.'

Jacob left them, and Joanna tried not to let the other woman's assumption of authority undermine her confidence. But her words had been in the nature of a reprimand, and it was apparent that Jacob regarded her instructions as law.

'Now . . .' The woman Jacob had called Camilla indicated a low armchair. 'Won't you sit down, Miss Carne? I'm sure we can speak much more amicably that way.'

Joanna took a deep breath. 'I prefer to stand.'

She didn't. But the small gesture of defiance did not go unnoticed as she had intended.

'Very well.' Camilla made an indifferent gesture. 'What brings you to Kwyana, Miss Carne?'

'I don't think that's anything to do with you,' replied Joanna evenly. 'And I'd like to ask some questions of my own, if you have no objections.'

'None at all.'

Camilla lounged gracefully into an armchair, crossing her long slender legs, and immediately Joanna felt at a disadvantage. The white uniform did something for the other woman, she had to admit, and she could quite see that Camilla would enjoy wearing it. It would command admiration and respect among the Africans, and was the perfect foil for her dark beauty.

Suddenly aware of her own dishevelled appearance when compared to that dusky elegance, Joanna broke into speech:

'What is wrong with my brother?'

Camilla's look was vaguely condescending. 'Malaria, Miss Carne. Your brother is recovering from an attack of malaria.'

'Is that serious?'

'It can be. But nowadays, with modern drugs and modern treatment, it is not the debilitating thing it once was. Nevertheless, it can be most unpleasant for the patient, as you saw.'

Joanna nodded. 'But is he getting better?'

'Well, he's not getting any worse,' Camilla amended dryly. 'Knowing your brother, I'd say he'd be up and about in a couple of days.'

'Oh, thank goodness!' Joanna could not hide her relief, but the other woman was regarding her frowningly.

'I—I understood Shannon broke with his family some years ago,' she ventured unexpectedly, and Joanna felt the hot colour fill her cheeks.

'Did you?' she managed, turning away towards the windows which overlooked the bungalow adjacent to this, noticing how the shadows were lengthening as the afternoon drew to its close. It would be dark soon. 'I—I'm very hungry,' she said quietly. 'Do you think Jacob would make me a sandwich? I haven't eaten since this morning.'

She was conscious of Camilla getting to her feet, and glanced round half apprehensively to find the other woman surveying her contemptuously. Without her controlled mask of composure she looked older than Joanna had first thought her, but no less intimidating.

'Shannon will not want you here,' she stated with cold conviction. 'I know how he feels about his—*family*!'

Joanna squared her shoulders. 'Do you? Well, I intend to stay and find that out for myself.'

'Then you're a fool!' Camilla controlled her sudden outburst, and with calmer emphasis, asked: 'Where do you intend to stay? There are no hotels here.'

Joanna gasped. 'I—shall stay here, naturally.'

'Where? There is only one bedroom. These bungalows are built for individuals, not for entertaining.'

Joanna looked about her. 'I can use two of these chairs, pushed together. You don't have to bother about me, Miss—Miss——?'

'Langley. Nurse Langley,' retorted Camilla abruptly. 'And you can't sleep here. There's no mosquito netting, and these chairs are probably infested with bugs. Or don't you care?'

Joanna hid her instinctive shiver of fear. Insects of any kind terrified her, but she refused to let Camilla see that. 'I'll manage somehow,' she insisted, clinging to the knowledge that this woman could not force her to leave.

'Why have you come here?'

Clearly her presence at Kwyana represented a problem to Camilla, but Joanna had no intention of satisfying her curiosity.

'I want to speak to Shannon,' she said steadily. 'Now, will you call Jacob, or shall I?'

That small piece of defiance brought an angry darkening of colour to Camilla's cheeks, but before either of them could speak again, someone knocked at the outer door and a man's voice, with a definite American accent, called: 'Is anybody home?'

Camilla's face cleared, and ignoring Joanna, she walked to the hall door, her smile warm and welcoming. 'I'm here, Brad,' she answered. 'Come on in.'

Footsteps sounded in the hall, and then a man appeared in the doorway, casually dressed in a bush shirt and shorts. He was a huge man, with broad shoulders and rusty hair that extended from his head, over his chest and down his arms and legs. Joanna guessed he wasn't much more than Shannon's age, and his bushy eyebrows ascended rapidly at sight of her.

'Hell's teeth, who's this?' he exclaimed, grinning. 'A

white female, no less. Shannon has all the luck!'

Camilla cast a denigrating glance in Joanna's direction. 'That is Shannon's sister,' she remarked briefly. 'Or so she says. I must say, she doesn't look much like him!'

'I am Shannon's sister!' declared Joanna hotly, and then coloured herself at the look in the American's eyes.

'I believe you,' he said, coming towards her holding out his hand. 'I'm Brad Steiner, ventilation superintendent at the mine. And you're ...?'

'Joanna. Joanna Carne. How do you do?' Joanna allowed him to envelop her small hand in his much larger one, and then withdrew her fingers quickly. 'Are you a friend of my brother's, Mr Steiner?'

'The name's Brad, and yes, I guess you could call me that. We're old buddies. Used to work together in the Transvaal. Came up to Lushasa at the same time.'

'I see.'

As Joanna absorbed this, Brad turned back to Camilla. 'Anyway, how is he?' he asked, with evident concern. 'That's why I came. Meeting Joanna ...' he used her name quite unselfconsciously, 'was just a bonus.'

'He's a little better,' replied Camilla shortly. She had not liked Brad's response to Joanna's fair attraction, and her smile was no longer in evidence. 'I've just been explaining to Miss Carne that she can't possibly stay here.'

Brad frowned. 'Stay here? Oh, you mean actually here, in Shannon's house?' He looked Joanna's way again. 'Shannon didn't mention you were coming, or we'd have fixed something up, wouldn't we, Camilla? As it is——'

'Shannon didn't know I was coming, Mr Steiner,' said Joanna reluctantly, aware of the other woman's contempt. 'It's a—surprise visit. And you really don't have to worry about me. I'll manage.'

'I think Miss Carne should be accommodated at the hospital,' put in Camilla, as Brad Steiner stood considering the situation, his brows drawn together. 'There are plenty of spare beds there, and it would avoid the inevitable speculation her arrival is bound to cause among the men.'

'You could be right——' Brad was beginning, when Joanna broke in angrily.

'I have no intention of sleeping at the hospital,' she exclaimed. 'I've already told Miss—Nurse Langley. I'm staying here.'

'Sleeping on two chairs!' Camilla was scornful.

'Have you a better suggestion?' countered Joanna, but Brad raised his hand in protest.

'I have,' he said with finality. 'I have that folding camper my nephew Rod used when he visited last year. Providing the bugs haven't eaten it away, you could use that, Joanna.'

Joanna wasn't quite sure what a camper was, but she guessed it was some sort of folding bed. 'That would be marvellous!' she thanked him, but Camilla still had an objection.

'What about the mosquitoes?' she demanded.

'I guess I have some netting somewhere,' Brad assured her, his eyes twinkling at Joanna. 'Like the lady says, we'll manage.'

'I shall have to report this to Doctor Reisbaum,' stated Camilla shortly, and marched out of the room.

After she had gone there was an uneasy silence, and then Brad grinned at Joanna, and some of the tension left her. 'Don't mind Camilla,' he said. 'Like all medical people, she thinks we ordinary mortals don't know how to look after ourselves. But she's a damn good nurse, and she'd do anything for Shannon, you know.'

'I know.' Joanna had gathered that, but she had her own interpretation of Camilla's motives. Camilla didn't want her here, but it was a much more personal thing than caring for Shannon's health. She had made that very plain.

'I live next door,' Brad was saying now, and Joanna dragged her thoughts back to the present. 'What say I go round, get my houseboy to fetch you the camper and set it up in here while you wash up, then maybe later you'd come round and have supper with me?'

Joanna plucked the damp denim away from her midriff, looking doubtful. She longed to submerge her sticky limbs in cool water, but the idea of taking supper with this friendly American did not appeal. What she really had in mind was to wash and change her clothes, cajole Jacob into making her something to eat, and then sit with Shannon for a while. Even if he wasn't aware of her presence, it would give her time to collect her thoughts.

'I really think I'd rather stay here this evening,' she refused him politely. 'I'm grateful for your offer of the bed, but I am rather—tired.'

Brad nodded understandingly. 'Okay. Point taken. I'll have Andy fetch the camper round in a few minutes.' He walked towards the door and then paused. 'If you have any trouble with Jacob, just let me know.'

Which wasn't very reassuring, Joanna thought, but she saw Brad to the door, and then walked down the hall looking for the kitchen. It wasn't difficult to find. Someone had switched on the strip lighting, and when she paused in the doorway she saw that Jacob was sitting on a tall stool beside a steel-covered working surface, studying the newspaper which was spread out in front of him. There was no sign of Camilla, and Joanna looked round the small, functional room with interest. Because of the incidence of electricity, everything was extremely modern and up to date, even to the presence of a deep freeze in one corner.

Clearing her throat to attract the African's attention, she said: 'Could you tell me where the bathroom is, Jacob?'

Jacob looked round, and because her eyes were steady and inquiring, he got reluctantly to his feet. 'You staying here, miss?' he asked, a certain amount of aggression in his tone.

Joanna sighed. 'Yes.'

'That's what Miss Camilla said.'

'Good.' Joanna glanced round. 'Where is—Miss Camilla?'

'She's gone. Back to hospital.' Jacob's chin jutted. 'Who say you stay here? This Mr Carne's house.'

Joanna gasped. 'And I'm Mr Carne's sister!' she retorted, angrily. 'Are you questioning my right to be here, Jacob?'

Jacob's belligerence suffered a slight puncturing. 'Miss Camilla, she say better you stay at hospital.'

'I don't give a damn what Miss Camilla says!' Joanna answered furiously. 'I'm staying here, and if you have any objections, I suggest you save them until your employer is capable of answering them himself!'

'Yes'm,' mumbled Jacob sullenly, and then: '*Mr Carne*, sir!'

Joanna had been too taken up with her argument with Jacob to be aware of any sound behind her, but the horrified look on Jacob's face made her swing round in dismay, her lips parting involuntarily. Somehow Shannon had dragged himself out of bed, pulled on a navy bathrobe which he had wrapped loosely about him, and was standing swaying behind her. He was no less pale than when she had seen him tossing on his bed, but at least his eyes had lost their glazed stare.

'For heaven's sake, Jacob,' he was saying, grasping the door post for support, 'what in hell is going on?' Then his eyes shifted to Joanna, and she saw the wave of disbelief that crossed his lean features. 'My God! It *was* you!' he muttered incredulously. 'I—thought I was dreaming!'

Joanna could feel a lump in her throat just looking at him, and her voice was unsteady as she said softly: 'Yes, it's me, Shannon. I'm—I'm sorry you're not well.'

'Not well!' Shannon raised his eyes heavenward for a moment. 'For God's sake, what are you doing here?' His eyes darted round the room. 'Who brought you? You can't have come alone.'

'I did. But it doesn't matter about that right now.'

Joanna came towards him, touching the hand that held his robe in place. 'You're shivering, Shannon. You shouldn't be out of bed.'

Shannon flinched away from her touch, and she felt a shaft of pain go through her. 'I'm all right,' he muttered abruptly. 'But you shouldn't be here. Why have you come? Does—does your father know you're travelling alone?'

'Yes. Oh, yes.' Joanna spread her hands. 'Shannon, please—go back to bed. We can't talk like this.'

She glanced meaningly towards Jacob, and Shannon looked at the African. 'What's going on, Jacob?' he demanded sharply. 'Why were you arguing with—Miss Carne when I came on the scene?'

Jacob looked uneasy. 'Miss Carne, she want to stay here. Miss Camilla say she stay at hospital,' he related defensively.

Shannon's jaw muscles tightened. 'I see.' He looked again at Joanna. 'That's quite a point.'

Joanna felt near to tears. 'Oh, don't you start, please,' she begged. 'Mr Steiner—Brad—he's offered me the use of a camp bed, and I'm perfectly capable of taking care of myself. I don't even need Jacob to make me something to eat. I can cook. I'm not helpless.'

Shannon's brow furrowed. 'You're hungry?'

'A little.'

'When did you last eat?'

'Oh—this morning——'

'This *morning*!' Shannon sounded impatient, but his stamina was waning. His knuckles were white where they held on to the door, and Joanna risked another rebuff by saying:

'Leave it to me, Shannon. Go back to bed. You're ill. Let me handle this.'

Lines of strain were etched beside his mouth, but still he remained. 'Miss Carne needs a bath and a change of clothes, Jacob,' he ordered grimly. 'While she's attending to herself, you can prepare her a meal, is that understood?'

Jacob nodded, with ill grace. 'Yes'm, Mr Carne.'

'And if I hear of you behaving disrespectfully again, you're fired, is that clear?'

'Yes'm, Mr Carne.'

Shannon expelled his breath wearily. 'Good.' He released the door post and stood swaying unsteadily. 'God—this damned disease! Why did it have to happen now?'

He staggered, and to Joanna's astonishment, before she could do anything, Jacob had rushed past her and supported her brother back to his room. After the dressing down he had just received, Joanna would have expected Jacob to ignore his master's weakness, maybe even enjoy it, but it was obvious from the way he behaved that he cared what happened to him. Her own shoulders sagged. What a day it had been, and it wasn't over yet.

The bathroom Jacob showed her to had a bath and a shower, but Joanna decided to use the former. It was heaven to soak her limbs in the tepid, slightly brackish water which emitted from the taps, and afterwards she washed her hair and wound it up in a towel. She had clean clothes in her overnight case, but only one set, and she realised she would have to wash out the clothes she had just taken off so that they would be fit to wear the following day. However, Jacob came tapping at the bathroom door as she was rubbing her hair dry to tell her that her supper was waiting, and she decided to leave washing her clothes until later.

The meal that awaited her smelt very appetising. Jacob had served it on the formica-topped table in the kitchen, and he disappeared while she was eating so that she felt no self-consciousness. Tinned soup was followed by fried chicken and rice, and there was a bowl of fruit to finish. There was cheese, too, but it smelt rather strong, and Joanna had no desire to risk an upset stomach.

While she ate, a steady stream of insects flung themselves suicidally at the window panes, endeavouring to reach the light, and Joanna instinctively turned her back on them. The soft velvety wings and hairy legs sent a crawling sensation up her spine, and she prayed none of them would gain entrance without her knowledge.

A percolator was bubbling on the stove, and she was helping herself to a cup of coffee when Jacob came back. Summoning a smile, she said: 'That was delicious, thank you.'

Jacob regarded her doubtfully for a few moments, and then he said: 'You really Mr Carne's sister, hmm?'

'That's right.'

He nodded, as though satisfied by her answer. 'Mr Steiner's boy came with the bed,' he added. 'We put it in living room, yes?'

'That sounds fine.' Joanna finished her coffee and put the cup down. 'Er—is Mr Carne sleeping?'

Jacob raised his eyebrows. 'Maybe, maybe not. Missus go see.'

'But—the dishes——'

'Jacob see to dishes,' he told her, in as amiable a tone as she had heard from him. 'You want anything, you ask Jacob.'

Joanna shook her head. Obviously Shannon's reproof had been taken to heart, but she guessed that when Camilla returned Jacob's loyalties might well divide again.

Leaving the kitchen, she crossed the hall to the bathroom to collect her dirty clothes. But the bathroom was empty of her belongings and she looked round in dismay. Where had they gone? Surely Jacob hadn't shifted them.

Crossing back to the kitchen, she hovered in the doorway, watching the houseboy as he loaded her dirty dishes into the sink. 'Er—Jacob?' she murmured tentatively. 'Do you happen to know where the things are that I left in the bathroom?'

Jacob turned, his black hands incongruously covered with white soap suds. 'Sure thing, missus. They washed. Jacob put them by your bed.'

Joanna shook her head. 'I don't understand . . .'

'Jacob use washing machine and drier. While you have supper.' He looked anxious. 'Jacob do wrong?'

'Oh, no.' Joanna couldn't prevent a smile from lifting the corner of her mouth. 'I—well, thank you, Jacob. Thank you.'

She turned away and went along the hall to the living room. The room was in darkness, but she switched on the light and started at the tentlike erection of mosquito netting which had been rigged over the canvas bed. But sure enough, her clothes were there, somewhat creased perhaps, but freshly laundered. With a rueful smile, she left the room again, switching out the light as she went.

Shannon's door was ajar, and through the crack she could see a lamp had been lighted beside his bed. She pushed the door a little wider, wincing as it squeaked a little, and looked in. At first she thought he was asleep, but he had heard her because he turned his head against the pillows, and said harshly: 'You'd better come in.'

CHAPTER THREE

JOANNA closed the door behind her and leaned back against it for a moment. 'How—how do you feel?' she asked automatically.

'Lousy!' Shannon ran a hand across his forehead, brushing back the thick hair carelessly. 'Joanna, what the hell are you doing here?'

Joanna straightened away from the door and approached the bed. 'I came to see you,' she answered simply.

'For God's sake, why?' His eyes were dark amber in the shadowy light, his skin brown and oiled with sweat. 'Joanna, I broke with—with the family ten years ago. There was no reason for you to come here—'

'Yes, there was.' She was standing beside the bed now, and she twisted her hands tightly together as she looked down at him. She had been an adolescent when he went away, and the things she had noticed about him then, were not the things she was noticing now. Since his departure, she had grown up, had known the touch of a man's lips, the urgency of his caresses, and she could understand only too well why Camilla Langley regarded any woman as a threat where Shannon was concerned. He was disturbingly attractive, even in this weakened state, and Joanna went cold when she realised what she was thinking.

Stepping back from the bed, she hastened into speech: 'Daddy—Daddy's had a stroke,' she got out jerkily. 'A massive stroke, the doctors say, and he's partially paralysed because of it.'

Shannon's face registered no visible emotion, but it was several moments before he said: 'What has that to do with me?'

Joanna took a deep breath, and as she warmed to her cause it was easier to forget her feelings of a few moments ago. 'He wants to see you, Shannon. He wants to talk to you. He wants you to come back to England—'

'*No!*'

'Why not?' There was desperate appeal in her voice. 'Oh, Shannon, you don't know what it's been like. Mummy's half out of her mind with worry, and the doctors say that if Daddy has a second stroke——' She broke off, biting her lower lip. 'You know what it would mean.'

'It's not my concern.'

Shannon was looking straight ahead, not at her, and his profile was hard and unyielding.

'You don't mean that!' she exclaimed disbelievingly.

'I do.' His hands clenched on the sheet that covered him. 'My life is here, in Africa, in gold mining. I have no interest in anything else.'

Joanna caught her breath. 'I—I can't—I *won't* accept that.'

'You'll have to.'

Joanna forgot herself sufficiently to kneel on the floor beside the bed and take one of his hands between both of hers. But he wrenched his hand away, and ignominiously, she burst into tears. It had all been too much—the long complicated journey, the hostility which had awaited her here, at Kwyana, and now Shannon's utter rejection. It was so disappointing, and she buried her face in her arms and allowed the sobs which welled up inside her to shake her whole body.

'Oh, for the Lord's sake, Joanna!'

His feet appeared on the floor beside her, and he wrenched his bathrobe from the foot of the bed, thrusting his arms into the sleeves and wrapping it around him before hauling her up into his arms. Her face was pressed between the lapels of the robe, against the curling dark hair which covered that area of his chest, and her mouth and nostrils

35

were filled with the taste and the smell of him. He held her closely until her sobs subsided, and she felt a wonderful sense of security in his arms. But when she lifted her face to look at him, he pushed her almost roughly away and sank down weakly on to the side of the bed.

'It's no use, Joanna,' he said harshly. 'You're wasting your time here. I will not be coming back to England.'

Joanna rubbed her wrists across her cheeks, and saw his eyes narrow as they alighted on the solitaire diamond which occupied the third finger of her left hand. Ignoring the query in his eyes, she exclaimed: 'Why not? Don't you care about us any more?'

Shannon lay back wearily against the pillows. 'That's a futile question. My feelings are not involved. When I left the estate, your father knew I would never come back.'

'Unless he begged you to do so!' protested Joanna desperately.

'Is that what he's doing?' Shannon turned scornful eyes in her direction. 'Sending you to plead his case?'

'He couldn't come himself!' she cried. 'Don't you understand? He'll never walk again! And if necessary, I'll beg, Shannon. I'm not proud!'

'Unfortunately, I am.'

'Oh, Shannon, please! Don't send me home alone!'

Joanna was extending an appealing hand towards him when after the briefest of warnings, Camilla Langley let herself into the room. Immediately, Joanna's hand fell to her side and she turned away, self-consciously aware of the tear stains on her cheeks, and her still-damp hair tumbling untidily from the topknot in which she had secured it. Her purple jeans and matching denim shirt looked boyish beside Camilla's voluptuous elegance, the other woman having shed her uniform in favour of a slim-fitting shift of yellow silk which moulded every inch of her curving body. Joanna wished she had brought a dress to wear, but her clothes still lay in the suitcase at the hotel in Menawi.

Ignoring the girl, Camilla approached the bed, frowning when she realised Shannon had been out of it. Taking his wrist between her fingers, she checked his pulse rate, and then cast an impatient look in Joanna's direction.

'I thought you would have more sense than to upset your brother, Miss Carne,' she stated coldly. 'I warned you that you should stay away from him until he was recovered.'

'Oh, come on, Camilla!' muttered Shannon irritably, before Joanna could reply. 'I'm not an invalid. As a matter of fact, I intend going back to work in a couple of days.'

'That would be very foolish!' Camilla put her hands on her hips. 'There's nothing going on at the mine that requires your personal attention. I hear that Douglas Forbes is managing very well.'

'Do you? Well, I'll decide when I go back to work, thank you.' Shannon levered himself up on his elbow. 'If you've come to stick needles into me, let's get it over with, shall we?'

Camilla compressed her lips. 'When Miss Carne has left us,' she said.

Shannon sighed and looked at Joanna. 'Yes, Jo, you'd better leave us,' he agreed heavily. 'Go get some sleep. We'll talk again in the morning.' He paused. 'Before you leave.'

His message was loud and clear, and a triumphant, provocative smile curved Camilla's lips. But Joanna chose not to listen. With a muffled exclamation, she crossed the room and let herself out of the door, not even trusting herself to tell him goodnight.

The living room was in darkness, and she switched on the light and went inside, closing the door behind her. Someone, she guessed it had been Jacob, had left her a glass of iced lime juice beside her bed, a cover protecting it from dust and insects. At the windows, the barrage of moths began again with the appearance of the light, and with a sigh she went and drew the blinds, too weary to pay them much attention.

As she undressed, she refused to think about tomorrow. Tiredness was taking its toll of her, and all she wanted was to crawl between the sheets and seek oblivion in sleep. Circumstances always seemed that much blacker at night, not least the knowledge of her awareness of Shannon. But when he had held her in his arms, she had wanted to stay there, and getting that reaction into perspective was not an easy thing to do.

The possibility of the failure of her mission was something she had not considered up till now. Until this evening she had felt convinced that once he knew the facts of the situation, Shannon could not fail to respond to them. He must remember what a proud and virile man their father had been, tall and upright, how he had loved walking and riding, physical pursuits of all kinds. To be deprived of everything in one cruel blow should arouse some compassion in his son. Shannon's bitterness and rejection seemed out of all proportion after all these years, and she could hardly believe that the row they had had was wholly responsible for the way Shannon felt now.

She put on the cotton nightdress she had brought with her, its narrow straps showing white against her creamy shoulders. Releasing her hair from the pins, she allowed it to tumble about her shoulders in silky disorder, running combing fingers through its length, too tired to get out her brush and do it properly. She ached with weariness and even the narrow bed looked inviting. Before putting out the light, she folded back the netting and pulled down the sheet. The enormous cockroach which had been imprisoned by the cover ran wildly across the bed to escape her, and Joanna had to stifle the scream that rose in her throat.

Picking up a sandal, she knocked the revolting creature to the floor, and then quickly ground the sandal into it. The awful crunching sound it made caused a sickly bile to enter her mouth, but nothing would have induced her to call

38

for assistance. Even so, the idea of getting between sheets where the beetle had lain filled her with distaste, and only the awareness of Camilla Langley's presence prevented her from asking Jacob for fresh bedding. Nevertheless, she examined every inch of the bed before extinguishing the light, and even after she was lying between the sheets, her thoughts constantly summoned images of giant beetles and spiders invading this ground floor room, crawling over her as she slept. She thought with longing of her room back home, a large comfortable room, with a sloping roof and a window set beneath the eaves. It was similar to the room she and Philip would share at his home after they were married in June. His parents were due for retirement, and when she and Philip returned from their honeymoon, they intended to move into a comfortable bungalow they had bought near Keswick, leaving Philip to run the farm. Thinking of Philip was reassuring somehow. She had not thought a lot about him since coming to Africa, and not at all since her arrival in Kwyana. She wondered what Shannon would think of Philip, or indeed what Philip would think of her half-brother. They had never met. The Lawsons had bought their farm after Shannon had left home. And if he continued to refuse to come to England, they might never meet.

Eventually Joanna slept, exhaustion temporarily erasing her anxieties about her surroundings, and not even the rain which came drumming on the corrugated roof in the early morning aroused her.

When she did awaken it was broad daylight. Someone had unkindly opened the blinds, and the sunlight slatting across her eyes was distracting. She rolled over drowsily, and saw a man's legs encased in close-fitting denims only inches away from her face.

Her eyes widened and travelled slowly upward over muscular thighs, a low buckled belt, to a denim shirt open almost to the waist, and finally reached Shannon's darkly tanned features. His eyes were narrowed as he looked down at her, but he looked better this morning. His face was still pale beneath his tan, but some of the strain had disappeared from around his eyes. His scrutiny made Joanna aware that the sheet had worked its way down to her waist, and the upper part of her body was only thinly concealed beneath the cotton nightgown. She grasped the sheet and dragged it over her, and he moved away from the bed, walking indolently towards the windows.

'Did you sleep well?' he inquired, with controlled politeness, and Joanna rolled on to her back and nodded.

'Eventually. Did you?' She propped herself up on one elbow. 'Ought you to be out of bed?'

Shannon leant against the window sill. 'Are you aware of the time?' he countered.

Joanna shook her head and reached for her watch. The hands indicated twenty minutes to ten and she gasped. 'Is it really so late?'

'Really,' he acknowledged sardonically. 'We rise early around here. I'm normally at the mine by seven.'

'But you were ill,' she protested, frowning. 'Did—did Nurse Langley give you permission to get up?'

'I don't need permission,' he retorted, straightening. 'Now, do you want some breakfast? Jacob's scrambled eggs are not unpalatable, and he makes a decent cup of coffee.'

'I know. I had some last night.' Joanna sat upright, holding the sheet firmly under her chin. 'Shannon,' she began, as the reasons for her being here began to assert themselves again. 'Shannon, you didn't mean——'

'I'll tell Jacob you'll be ready to eat in twenty minutes,' Shannon interrupted her, walking towards the door. 'There's a train leaving for Menawi at three o'clock this afternoon, and I expect you to be on it.'

The door slammed behind him, and Joanna hunched her shoulders dejectedly. He couldn't mean it, she told herself vehemently, but she remained unconvinced.

Wrapping the sheet around her, she carried her clothes

40

to the bathroom, and showered and cleaned her teeth before getting dressed. Then she went back to the living room, pushed her nightdress and the clothes Jacob had washed for her into her overnight case, and brushed her hair. It hung thick and straight about her shoulders, and she left it that way, even though it was really too heavy to wear loose in this climate.

Jacob was in the kitchen when she appeared, and he greeted her cheerfully as he set a plate of scrambled eggs and bacon in front of her. It was not what she was used to, but she hadn't the heart to disillusion him, and made a gallant effort to enjoy it. The coffee helped it down, and she drank several cups.

'Jacob go and clear away bed,' he announced, once he was sure she had everything she needed, but Joanna stopped him.

'Not yet, Jacob,' she said, putting down her fork. 'By the way, there—there was a bug in my bed last night.'

Jacob's horror was not pretended, she was sure of it. 'There no bugs in those sheets when Mr Steiner's boy and me make bed!' he insisted indignantly. 'Why you not call Jacob and have him change sheets?'

Joanna shook her head. 'I didn't want to—bother anyone last night. But if I happen to stay tonight, do you think I could have some fresh bedding?'

'You won't be staying tonight,' retorted Shannon's deep voice from the doorway, and she turned to stare resentfully at him.

'You can't force me to leave today!' she exclaimed. 'Why should I? I've only just got here. Why shouldn't I stay and see something of the place?'

'Kwyana is not a holiday resort!' replied Shannon cuttingly. His eyes lifted to the houseboy. 'You can strip down the camper, Jacob, and take it back to Mr Steiner's boy. We won't be needing it again.'

Joanna's breath caught in the back of her throat, and she

41

pushed back her chair and got unsteadily to her feet. 'You —you *pig*!' she burst out tremulously. 'You won't even consider what I told you, will you?'

Jacob was listening to their exchange with wide troubled eyes, but Shannon snapped his fingers angrily at him. 'What are you hanging about for?' he demanded, and mumbling an apology the boy left them alone.

Joanna pushed her plate aside, the eggs barely half eaten, staring down at the table through a mist of tears. So that was that. Shannon was forcing her to leave, and she felt more devastated now than she had when she had first learned of her father's stroke. But why should she care? she asked herself angrily. Her father would be disappointed, but it was not the end of the world. So why did she feel so shattered by it all?

Shannon uttered an oath suddenly, and came to stand wearily at the other side of the table, supporting himself with his palms against its cool surface, staring at her half angrily. 'God, Joanna, it's no use you staying here, hoping I'll change my mind!'

Joanna stole a look at him. His brow was beaded with sweat even though the room was comparatively cool, and she realised with an anxious pang that he was still suffering the after-effects of his illness.

'It—it doesn't occur to you that I might like being here, that I might like being with you, does it?' she asked quietly.

Shannon straightened, thrusting his hands deep into the pockets of his jeans. 'No.'

'Why not? Shannon, we haven't seen one another for ten years! I—I've missed you. I missed you terribly when you first went away, and then never hearing from you— never really knowing what you were doing. Surely it's not unreasonable that I should want to talk to you, should want to hear what's been happening to you?' She traced the pattern of the formica with a fingernail. 'I can't believe you don't have any feelings about us!'

42

Shannon wiped the sweat from his forehead, and then raked a hand through his hair in a defeated gesture. 'Why did he send you!' he muttered, half to himself.

Joanna's eyes widened. 'Who else could have come? Mummy's nerves are in a dreadful state. There was no one else. I—I had to try.'

Shannon turned away, his facial muscles tightening. 'Well, I suppose I can't blame you for that.'

Joanna sighed, and risking a rebuff she went round the table to him, sliding her arm through his. He stiffened and would have drawn away, the muscles of his arm taut against her skin. But she held on to him, aware as she did so that she was risking more than his anger. 'What's happened, Shannon?' she asked, rushing into speech. 'Why are you being like this? Can't you forget the past as Daddy has done?'

Shannon looked down at her, and the torment in his eyes sent a forbidden shiver up her spine. When he looked at her like that it was very hard to hang on to her identity. 'Do you think he has?' he demanded huskily. 'Forgotten the past, I mean? I don't. I think he hates me just as much as he ever did, only now there's very little he can do about it! Except send you here—with that ring on your finger!'

'Shannon!' Joanna was aghast. 'Daddy doesn't hate you!'

Shannon drew his hand out of his pocket so unexpectedly, that she almost lost her balance, and she wrapped her arms about herself defensively as she faced him. 'Oh, yes, he does, Joanna,' he told her violently, swaying a little as he spoke. 'And you can tell him I feel exactly the same!'

'Shannon! Shannon, why?'

Joanna's lips parted in dismay as his hands descended on her shoulders, gripping her almost cruelly, and shaking her as he spoke. 'Are you really as naïve as you appear?' he asked harshly, staring penetratingly at her. 'Don't you know anything about the reasons why I left England?'

Joanna licked her dry lips. 'I—you had a row with

Daddy.'

'Is that all?'

'It—it was something to do with—with your mother, wasn't it?' she ventured tentatively.

'My *mother*!' He raised his eyes heavenward for a moment. 'Oh, yes, it had to do with my mother.' He paused, his eyes raking her ruthlessly. 'But it had to do with you, too. Did no one ever tell you that?'

'No.' Joanna shook her head.

Shannon's lips twisted. 'No. No, of course they wouldn't.' He thrust her away from him, putting some distance between them. 'And you never guessed?'

'No.' Joanna was confused. 'What—what did I do?'

Shannon massaged the muscles at the back of his neck. 'God, my head aches!' he muttered, obviously impatient of his weakness. Then; 'Oh, don't look like that, Joanna. You didn't *do* anything. But you were there. And so was I. And our relationship ... Well, do you need me to draw a picture?'

'*No*!' Joanna put a horrified hand to her throat. 'You don't mean——'

'Don't pretend you're not aware of it, Joanna,' he said, savagely. 'It's been there between us ever since you came here yesterday, and if you're honest with yourself, you'll admit it. But there's no future in it. There never was. Your father took damn good care of that. But don't ask me to forget, because I know I won't.'

'You can't mean ...' Her voice shook and then trailed away.

'Oh, but I can. Everything. Everything, Joanna.' He turned away as though he couldn't stand the sight of her. 'I wasn't much more than a boy myself, but I——' He shook his head. 'Don't worry. I learned my lesson well. You have nothing to fear from me.'

Joanna was trembling. She knew she ought to feel ashamed, that she should be disgusted by what she had just

44

heard, but she wasn't. And that was the frightening part. Whatever he did, she knew she would never despise Shannon. And this explained so much—and yet left so much unexplained. And their father had sent her here, fully aware of what had happened in the past! Who could blame Shannon for despising him?

Taking a deep breath, she said: 'I—I'm sorry.' It was inadequate, but she was too stunned to say more.

He looked round at her. He had himself in control again, but he was paler than before and the sweat was rolling off him. He was feverish, she knew, but when she attempted to suggest that he should rest, he ignored her, and said: 'You're engaged, then? To anyone I know?'

Joanna shook her head. Philip represented sanity. 'No,' she got out. 'His name's Philip Lawson. His parents bought High Stoop.'

Shannon nodded, pressing his knuckles to his temples. 'Is he a farmer, too? I imagine he must be if he's won your father's approval.'

'Yes.' Joanna took a step towards him, stopping at the look in his eyes. 'Oh, Shannon—you're ill! You must go back to bed. Let me—help you.'

'I'm all right,' he muttered impatiently, straddling a chair and sitting down, resting his arms along its back and his head on his arms.

'You're not all right,' insisted Joanna, staring at him frustratedly. Then she walked to the door and shouted: 'Jacob! Jacob, come here!'

The houseboy came hurrying along the hall and judging by his expression Joanna guessed that he imagined their argument had erupted into violence. His face cleared when he saw Shannon and muttering to himself he came into the room.

'Mr Carne should be in bed,' stated Joanna firmly, ignoring the angry remonstrance this aroused. 'Will you help me, Jacob?'

'I can walk,' muttered Shannon, getting unsteadily to his feet, and refusing her assistance, he allowed Jacob to help him to his room.

After they had gone, Joanna paced restlessly about the kitchen. What to do now? Shannon had insisted that she must leave, but right now he was in no fit state to enforce that order. Besides, how could she go and leave him like this? She cared about him too much to abandon him, even to the undoubtedly expert ministrations of Camilla Langley, and always at the back of her mind there was the hope that he might change his mind. In spite of everything.

But one thing was certain. She could not remain at Kwyana with only one change of clothes. She needed the suitcase she had left at the hotel in Menawi, and there was only one way to get it. She would have to go back in the train this afternoon, stay at the hotel overnight, and return here tomorrow. But how was she to get to the railway station?

Jacob came back while she was worrying this problem, and she looked at him anxiously. 'Is—is Mr Carne in bed?'

Jacob nodded. 'Yes'm, he in bed. He not good patient. Miss Camilla say so.'

'Does she?' Joanna's tone was dry. 'Is there anything I can do for him?'

'No'm.' Jacob shook his head. 'He sleep for while. Miss Camilla come again later.'

'I suppose so.' Joanna did not relish the prospect of meeting the nurse again. 'Er—Jacob? How could I get to the railway station this afternoon?'

Jacob frowned. 'To railway station, missus? You leaving?'

'Temporarily,' said Joanna. Then changed it to: 'Just for a while. I'll probably be back tomorrow.'

Jacob shrugged. 'I take you to station. Jacob good chauffeur,' he announced with dignity.

Joanna gasped. 'I didn't realise you drove, Jacob. I'm

sorry. Does Mr Carne have transport?'

'Yes'm, he have station wagon. Parked out back. You want to see?'

'All right.'

Joanna nodded, and followed the houseboy through a door at the far side of the kitchen which opened into a narrow passage. Jacob indicated that this was the storeroom on one side of the passage and his own living quarters at the other. Then they emerged through a second door into the brilliant sunshine at the back of the house.

The first thing that Joanna noticed was the smell, a rich earthy smell of dampness and rotting vegetation. She guessed there had been rain during the night, but now everything was drying out rapidly, and mist rose from the hedges that gave the settlement an air of permanence. There was a stubby lawn at the back of the bungalow, and beyond this the rugged sides of the valley rose in rocky formation. It was a bare, desolate landscape, and she thought she preferred the row of bungalows, ugly though they appeared.

A dust-smeared Chrysler station wagon, a big comfortable vehicle stood to one side of the building on a stretch of concrete laid for the purpose. Jacob patted the car with obvious pride, jumping on to the fender to demonstrate its easy suspension. Then he opened all the doors and windows, squealing when his hands encountered red-hot metal.

'You like?' he asked, and smiling ruefully she nodded.

'It's huge, isn't it?' she commented, looking inside at the leather interior. 'How many gallons does it do to the mile?'

Jacob's brows came together as he puzzled this. 'How many gallons ...' he echoed confusedly, and she shook her head.

'I was only joking,' she apologised. 'No, really, it's very impressive—er—' this as Jacob looked perplexed again, '—I mean, it's a beautiful car.'

This satisfied him, and feeling the sun beating down mercilessly on her bare head, Joanna made for the coolness of the passage. She would pack her belongings and be ready to leave right after lunch.

Jacob had dismantled the mosquito netting and stripped the sheets off the camper, but the bed had not been folded away, and she made a mental note to ask him to leave it where it was. Her few belongings took no packing, and she was endeavouring to swallow some of the tinned pork and beans Jacob had prepared for her lunch when Camilla arrived. Joanna's appetite seemed to have dwindled alarmingly since coming to Kwyana, and the nurse's presence did not stimulate it.

Camilla offered an indifferent greeting and then summoned Jacob to accompany her. No doubt they were going to see the patient, but Joanna could feel herself stiffening so long as that woman was in the house. She had to steel herself to remain seated at the table, and when Jacob came back alone, she breathed a sigh of relief.

'Has—has she gone?' she queried, in what she hoped was a casual tone, and Jacob nodded solemnly.

'Yes'm.'

'Er—what did she say?'

He shrugged his bony shoulders. 'Nothing much. She come back later.'

Joanna frowned. Did she imagine it, or was there a trace of Jacob's earlier hostility in his behaviour? She couldn't be absolutely sure, but Camilla was not one to waste her opportunities, and she must have noticed how amicably Joanna and the houseboy were getting on together.

She finished eating and pushed her plate aside. 'That was very nice, Jacob, but I'm honestly not hungry. I'll just have some coffee, if I may?'

'Yes'm.'

Jacob attended to the percolator and Joanna watched him frustratedly. She had not been mistaken. Jacob was being abrupt, and a feeling of helplessness swept over her. She was leaving in an hour, leaving the field free for Camilla to cor-

48

rupt the boy's mind in whatever way she chose, and there was nothing she, Joanna, could do about it. She had hoped to leave here in a spirit of friendship, but obviously that was not going to be possible now.

Leaving Jacob to do the dishes, she went to say goodbye to Shannon. She intended telling him what she planned to do, and if he raised objections she would just ignore them.

But when she entered his bedroom, she found he was sound asleep, his breathing deep and stertorous. She hesitated waking him, but needs must, and bending over him, she said: 'Shannon! Shannon! Wake up! I have to talk to you.'

He did not stir, and with a sigh she touched the smooth skin of his shoulder, shaking him gently. Still he did not move, and the first twinges of alarm feathered along her spine.

'Shannon!' she said, more loudly now. 'Shannon, wake up! I'm leaving!'

His immobility frightened her, and she rushed out of the room and along to the kitchen, shouting for Jacob. She almost cannoned into him as he came to meet her, and she exclaimed breathlessly: 'Jacob, something's wrong with Mr Carne. I can't wake him!'

.For once there was no sign of concern in Jacob's dark eyes. 'Miss Camilla, she say he need rest,' he said, shrugging.

Joanna tried to interpret what he meant. 'You mean Miss Camilla's given him something to make him sleep?' she exclaimed in dismay.

'Yes'm.' Jacob mimed a needle going into his arm. 'Miss Camilla good nurse. She know best thing for Mr Carne.'

'Oh, *God*!' Joanna stared impotently at him, feeling tears of frustration pricking at her eyes. 'And I suppose Miss Camilla didn't know I was leaving,' she muttered bitterly.

'Yes'm, she knew. I told her myself.'

Joanna's shoulders sagged. 'But you knew I would want

49

to speak to him before I left. How could you let her do such a thing?'

Jacob's mouth curved sulkily. 'I not doctor. Miss Camilla don't ask me. You best speak with her.'

'I don't have time now.' Joanna clenched her fists. 'Oh, look—I'll write him a note. And you'd better see he gets it the minute he wakes up, right?'

Jacob turned away into the kitchen. 'I finish dishes. You leave note beside bed.'

Joanna pressed her lips together, and then sighed. Perhaps he was right. If she left the note beside Shannon's bed he would be sure to get it. Just now, Jacob wasn't really responsible for his actions.

CHAPTER FOUR

IT was late in the evening when the train pulled into Menawi station, and Joanna felt stiff and weary. But at least it was cooler in the capital, and there were taxis to take her to her hotel. Neon signs flashed from all the larger hotels and office buildings, and car horns honked endlessly. The streets they drove through were thronged with people out enjoying themselves, and the sound of western music mingled with the throbbing rhythm of the drums from nightclubs glittering along the main thoroughfares. It was all totally different from the remote mining settlement, and the aromas of spices and curries drifting through the open windows of the cab made Joanna realise how hungry she was.

She encountered Mr Krishna, the hotel's Asian manager, in the lobby when she went to collect her key, and he greeted her warmly.

'You have had a good trip to Kwyana, Miss Carne?' he inquired, with a polite smile. 'Myself I do not enjoy the trips up country.'

'It was—enlightening,' replied Joanna, with a slight smile. 'By the way, I shall be leaving again in the morning, Mr Krishna. My brother is living at Kwyana, and I intend to spend a few days with him before returning to England.'

Mr Krishna's narrow Asiatic features drew into a frown. 'You expect to return to Kwyana tomorrow, Miss Carne?'

'Why, yes.' Joanna looked troubled. 'Is something wrong? Oh—my belongings haven't been stolen or anything, have they?'

Mr Krishna looked wounded. 'This is a respectable hotel, Miss Carne. I cannot recall that anyone's luggage has been stolen from here.'

'I'm sorry.' Joanna mentally kicked herself for allowing Lorenz's malicious gossip to influence her. 'Well, what is it, then?'

'There are no trains to Kwyana tomorrow, Miss Carne. It's Sunday!'

'*Sunday!*' Joanna was aghast, but she knew with a sinking feeling that he was telling the truth. No wonder the streets of Menawi were filled with people! It was Saturday night, and that was the same the world over. 'I—I didn't think.'

If only she had!

'So you will be staying until Monday?' Mr Krishna prompted, his good humour partially restored.

'I—well, yes, I suppose I shall have to.' Joanna was trying to think, but it was difficult when her brain seemed to have stopped functioning. She took her key from the waiting receptionist and tucked it absent-mindedly into the pocket of her jeans. 'I'm afraid I've lost all count of the days.'

'It happens,' Mr Krishna assured her. 'And personally, I am delighted we are to have the pleasure of your company for an extra day.' He smiled again. 'Now, I am sure you must be tired and hungry. Can I order you something from the restaurant—to be sent up to your room, of course?'

Joanna watched as he summoned a boy to take up her case, and then made a helpless gesture. 'Perhaps—a sandwich?' she suggested. 'And some coffee.'

'Is that all?' Mr Krishna was disappointed. 'Can I not tempt you with the chicken which was on the menu this evening?'

As before at Kwyana, Joanna's hunger had deserted her, and she shook her head apologetically. All she could think of was that Jacob must have known that there were no trains on Sundays, but he had not chosen to tell her. And Shannon ... Well, Shannon didn't want her to go back.

'Perhaps a chicken sandwich,' she agreed, to please the

52

manager. 'But that's all.'

'Very well, Miss Carne. I'll attend to it at once.'

'Thank you.' The manager had turned away, when a thought occurred to her. 'Mr Krishna!' He turned back at once, his brows lifted expectedly. 'Mr Krishna, is there any way I could send a message to Kwyana?'

'I assume you mean before Monday?' he queried.

'Yes.'

Mr Krishna shook his head. 'Then no. The train carries all supplies, including the mail.'

'Are there no planes?'

'I believe the mining company owns a helicopter, Miss Carne, but there is nowhere for an aeroplane to land at Kwyana.'

'Oh!' Joanna nodded. 'Well, thank you.'

Her room was blessedly cool and dark, and after tipping the boy who had carried her case, she closed the door and flopped down wearily on to the bed. At least this bed had springs, she thought tiredly, kicking off her sandals and stretching her legs. Then her eyes alighted on the cream telephone beside the bed, her tiredness forgotten, she rolled on to her stomach and reached eagerly for the receiver.

The hotel operator was coolly polite. She was sorry, she said, but there were no lines to Kwyana. The telephones Joanna had seen there must have been internal communications. Joanna slammed down her receiver again, and buried her face in the silk coverlet.

Surprisingly, she slept quite well. But she had been very tired and the bed was more relaxing than the camper had been the night before. She awakened in the morning feeling infinitely brighter, and refused to worry about Shannon when for the next twenty-four hours there was nothing she could do about it.

She bathed and dressed in a lime green halter-necked dress, and went downstairs to take breakfast in the hotel

53

dining room. Potted plants and creeper-covered trellises divided the tables, and two talkative parrots with gorgeously coloured plumage kept the waiters informed of new arrivals from their perches by the door. Joanna smiled at their squawking, but she could quite see that someone with a hangover might not appreciate their exuberance.

As she waited for her coffee and rolls to be served, she looked through the windows to the tropical informality of the hotel gardens. Palms and eucalyptus trees formed a backcloth for more exotic plants, like the orange and purple bougainvillea which grew in such profusion over the stone arches of the cloister-like terrace which surrounded the hotel. Scarlet hibiscus and fragrant frangipani dripped between the polished leaves of a rubber plant, their life span measured in hours in this intense climate. Everything seemed more intense here, somehow; life, death, *emotion* . . .

'Miss Carne? Joanna? It is you, isn't it? I was sure I wasn't mistaken.'

Joanna's reverie was interrupted by the drawling American voice, and she swung round in surprise to find Brad Steiner, tall and bulky in a white tropical lounge suit, standing by her table.

Her lips parted involuntarily, and she forced a smile. 'Why, Mr Steiner! What are you doing here?' Then, as an awful thought struck her: 'Shannon's not worse, is he?'

Brad Steiner grinned ruefully. 'Not to my knowledge. He seemed okay when I left yesterday morning.'

'You left—yesterday morning?' Joanna tried to absorb what he was saying.

'Sure. I had a couple of days' leave, so I decided to take a trip down here. What about you?'

'I left—yesterday afternoon.' Joanna could see the waiter approaching with her tray. 'Well, it's been very nice meeting you again, Mr Steiner.'

'Hey now, is that a dismissal?' Brad moved aside as the waiter set the tray down on the table. 'There was I, about to suggest we took breakfast together, and you say a thing like that!'

Joanna took a deep breath. She didn't really feel like making small talk with anyone, but he had been kind enough to lend her his bed, and she knew it would be churlish to refuse.

'Please—do sit down,' she exclaimed, indicating the chair opposite. 'You'd better give your order now, or I'll be finished before you've even begun.'

'Thanks.' Brad lowered his bulk into the chair, and after checking what Joanna was eating, ordered the same. 'This is nice,' he commented, as the waiter went to attend to his needs. 'And so unexpected!' He frowned. 'I understood you intended spending several days with your brother.'

Joanna poured herself some coffee and nodded. 'I did. I *do*.' She paused. 'But my luggage was here, at the hotel, and I came down yesterday to collect it. I intended going back to Kwyana today, but as you probably know there are no trains on Sundays.'

Brad showed his comprehension. 'Of course, there aren't. So you're staying over until tomorrow?'

Joanna rested her elbows on the table, cradling her cup in her fingers. 'Yes. I'm hoping there's a train about nine-thirty.'

'The only train,' agreed Brad dryly, toying with a tea-spoon.

'The only train?' Joanna stared at him.

'That's right. It goes up to Kwyana in the morning, and comes back in the afternoon.' He considered her puzzled features. 'I came down by car. I shall be going back the same way. Want a lift?'

Joanna hesitated. 'I don't know,' she said doubtfully. 'Jacob will probably meet me off the train tomorrow afternoon.' But *would he*? And if not, how was she to get to the mine?

'That's okay,' Brad was saying expansively. 'Hell, I'll have you at Shannon's place long before Jacob needs to leave for the station.'

'It's very kind of you to offer, but . . .'

'. . . but you don't know me? I'm a stranger to you?'

'Well—yes.'

'So okay, let's spend the day together. Let's get to know one another. You said yourself you'd planned to leave today. You can't have made any plans yet.'

He was going too fast for her, and in her confused emotional state it was difficult to know how to handle him. It seemed unreasonable not to consider his suggestions when she had no real reason for refusing. And he had said he was a friend of Shannon's. But . . .

'I have to cable my father,' she said, buttering a warm roll. The butter had a slightly rancid taste, but after several days she was getting used to it. She spread the conserve thickly to disguise the taste of the butter, and added: 'And I have a letter to write to my fiancé.'

Brad's expression grew faintly sardonic. 'I had noticed the bauble,' he remarked offhandedly. 'Okay, point taken. You're engaged. I'm not suggesting we sleep together or anything. I just thought it might cheer both of us up to spend the day together. But if you don't like the idea, that's okay by me.'

'I didn't say that exactly,' said Joanna uncomfortably. 'Actually, I had thought of using the pool this morning.'

'Is that an invitation?'

'You're welcome to join me, if you like,' she offered, colouring a little, and Brad grinned his acceptance.

In spite of the heat, the water in the kidney-shaped pool was cool and refreshing. Around the pool, the patio area was bright with gaily coloured garden furniture, striped umbrellas shading glass-topped tables where ice chinked in buckets. Tall, frosted glasses were decorated with slices of lime or lemon, and button-black olives sprouted on cocktail sticks. The guests staying at the hotel were of various nationalities, many of them Europeans working in Lushasa in one capacity or another, and enjoying a weekend break in Menawi.

Joanna found she was glad of Brad's company. Everyone seemed to know someone, and without his comforting presence she would have felt rather isolated. As it was, he introduced her to two Germans he knew who were working on a hydro-electric scheme for the government, and they in turn introduced their wives, who lived in Menawi and only saw their husbands every other weekend. They were all interested to hear Joanna's reasons for visiting Lushasa, and she guessed that any stranger's presence created a welcome diversion.

The morning sped by, and after lunch, Joanna excused herself to send her cable and to write her letter to Philip. It was pleasant relaxing on her bed, listening to the buzz of conversation from the gardens beyond her windows, the sun slatted to a comfortable angle by the blinds.

Writing to Philip wasn't easy, she found. Although she had succeeded in part to put the things Shannon had told her to the back of her mind, composing a letter to Philip brought everything back into cold perspective. It was hard to write about her journey to Lushasa, to describe the country and its people, when her thoughts ricocheted from the remembrance of her childhood with Shannon in England, to that devastating confrontation at Kwyana. It was something out of the past, yet it had a distinct bearing on the present, and Joanna knew she had been deeply disturbed by it. But Philip was *her* reality, the kind and gentle man she was going to marry. The dangerous delights of forbidden fruit did not torment her. Somehow she had to make Shannon see that his future was more important than the past, that there was no earthly reason why he should not come home and take over the estate as her father so desperately wanted him to do. She would be married to Philip in four months' time.

A brief period to suffer her presence before being rid of her for good.

In the evening Joanna had dinner with Brad, and afterwards there was dancing in the hotel. All in all, it had been a relaxing day, and when he broached the subject of driving her back to Kwyana the next morning, she eventually agreed. Brad's car was bound to be more comfortable than the train, she thought, and besides, it was a long journey to make alone.

The first hundred miles of roadway leading to Kwyana was quite good. The country they passed through changed from dense bushland on the outskirts of Menawi to the open scrub she was used to seeing around the mine. At times the dust was choking, but at others, rain had moistened the ground, and that distinctive smell of earth and vegetation filled the car.

Soon after twelve, Brad stopped, and produced a flask of chilled beer and some ham sandwiches from the glove compartment. Joanna discovered that she was really hungry for once, and the alfresco meal was more enjoyable than the elaborate dinner they had shared the evening before. Watching her demolishing the last sandwich, Brad could not conceal his amusement.

'You sure do care about that brother of yours, don't you?' he exclaimed, not noticing the suddenly anxious look which crossed Joanna's face. 'I haven't seen you so animated since a couple of days ago at Kwyana. I guess absence does make the heart grow fonder, like they say. I only know my kid sister doesn't give a hoot about me!'

Joanna found the last mouthful of sandwich was sticking in her throat, and she took a mouthful of beer to shift it. Then she thanked Brad politely, and put the empty papers back into the glove compartment. Brad waited until she had finished, and then he gave her a wry look.

'Hey, did I say something wrong?' he asked, plaintively. 'You've gone all stiff on me again.'

Joanna forced herself to relax, and shook her head. 'I—well, you just reminded me about—Shannon,' she said. 'I—I wonder if he's better?'

'Camilla will have seen to that,' remarked Brad, starting the engine. 'You know she has quite a thing about your brother.'

'Does she?' Was that too abrupt? 'I—I didn't know.'

'Oh, sure thing. I thought you'd noticed.'

'And—and does my—my brother share her—feelings?'

Brad shrugged, reaching for a cigarette from a pack on the shelf in front of him. 'I guess he uses her, if you know what I mean. Heck, what man wouldn't, given half a chance? Women aren't too thick on the ground around Kwyana.'

Joanna turned her head to stare out of the side of the car. She had guessed, of course, but it sounded so much worse to hear it actually put into words. No wonder Nurse Langley took such a proprietorial interest in her patient! But did that give Camilla the right to be rude to her? And why should she treat her so?

The road had deteriorated into a series of cracks and potholes, and the heavy American car bounced violently on its springs, making Joanna feel a little sick as the beer and sandwiches were jostled together in her inside.

'Sorry about this,' said Brad, noticing her discomfort. 'It gets easier soon. We can cut across the veld, and shorten our journey by half a dozen miles.'

'Well, if you're sure ...' Joanna was saying doubtfully, when there was a terrific bang, and the steering wheel slewed dangerously through Brad's fingers. He grasped it tightly and applied his brakes, and the heavy car ground to a halt.

'Blow-out!' he told her, with a grimace. 'I'll have to change the wheel.'

Joanna bit back her own dismay, and climbed out with him to survey the mangled tyre. It was hardly surprising that they had had a puncture in these conditions, but they were still about fifty miles from their destination, she estimated, and the road did not look as though it got any better. What if they should have a second blow out?

Deciding there was no point in anticipating the worst, she squatted down beside Brad, watching while he jacked up the car, and then holding the nuts he unwound from the hub. It didn't take too long to fit the spare, but Brad was sweating freely in the heat, and when he had finished, he swallowed the last of the beer from the flask and smoked another cigarette before going on.

Joanna glanced surreptitiously at her watch and found it was already after two. There seemed little chance of them arriving at Kwyana in advance of the train now, and she gave up worrying about whether or not Jacob would go and meet her.

It was almost four when they intercepted the road which ran between the railway station and the mine, and Joanna was unutterably relieved to be able to identify her surroundings at last. Conversation had flagged since the incident with the tyre, and she had guessed that Brad was as anxious as she that they should arrive at the settlement with no further mishaps. They had seen no game on their journey, but once darkness fell it might be a different story, and Joanna expelled her breath on a sigh when they finally reached the outskirts of the mine settlement.

As they approached the bungalows, Joanna saw that Shannon's station wagon was parked outside, on the road. She wondered if that indicated that Jacob had been to the station to meet the train, or whether Shannon was well enough to have returned to work. Brad pulled up outside the adjoining bungalow, and Joanna thrust open her door and climbed out. She was thanking him for the lift, while he hoisted her cases and his own out of the boot, when Shannon came striding down his driveway.

Joanna's first thoughts were that he must obviously be

feeling better, but his face was as dark as a thundercloud, almost as dark as the black denim shirt and matching levis he was wearing. It was apparent that he was furiously angry about something, and she shifted uneasily from one foot to the other as he approached.

'I trust you had a pleasant journey?'

His first words were disconcerting, delivered in a danger-ously controlled tone, and Joanna found herself chewing at her lower lip. 'As a matter of fact, we had a puncture,' she told him, not quite able to meet his eyes. 'Er—didn't we, Brad?'

Brad had finished unloading the cases and slammed down the lid of the boot with a heavy thud. 'That's right,' he agreed. 'We did. Something really ought to be done about the road conditions around here.'

Shannon scarcely spared him a glance. His attention was concentrated on Joanna. 'I understand you intended com-ing back by train?' he said.

'I—well, yes, I did. But—but Brad was staying at the hotel, and he offered me a lift.' She made an apologetic gesture. 'I'm sorry if you've been worried. Did—did Jacob go to meet the train?'

'No,' replied Shannon flatly. 'I did.' He bent and picked up her cases. 'Shall we go?'

Joanna cast a helpless look in Brad's direction, and was rewarded by his reassuring wink. Then she slung her bag over her shoulder and hurried after Shannon up the con-crete driveway to his bungalow. He carried her cases into the hall, set them down, and then indicated the living room.

'In there,' he said. 'I want to talk to you.'

Joanna resented his tone, and flounced into the room. But when she swung round, ready to make some protest about his behaviour, she found she was alone. Pressing her lips together, she waited impatiently for him to come back. Was this a calculated attempt on his part to intimidate her? Did he imagine by keeping her waiting he would weaken

61

her indignation?

A lizard ran wildly across the wall beside her, and she started violently. But its presence made her aware of her surroundings and she realised in dismay that the camp bed had been removed. Then she remembered. In her annoyance over Shannon's sedation before she left, she had forgotten to countermand Jacob's instructions. She sighed. Did nothing go right for her? She was beginning to wonder why she had even bothered to come back here. She had spoken to Shannon, and failed to get his agreement to return to England. Her father could not expect more of her than that. Why hadn't she simply accepted Shannon's refusal and instead of returning to Kwyana, taken the first plane out of Menawi bound for England?

A sound behind her heralded Shannon's return, and she turned as he came into the room and closed the door behind him. But she was unable to sustain the penetration of his stare, and bending her head, she said peevishly: 'Was it necessary to be rude to Brad Steiner?'

'I don't recall being rude to him,' retorted Shannon coolly. 'As a matter of fact, I don't recall addressing him at all.'

'That's just the point,' said Joanna, lifting her head. 'There is such a thing as dumb insolence, you know.'

'Is there?' Shannon's heavy lids narrowed his eyes. 'There is also thoughtlessness, incompetence, and a careless disregard for anyone's feelings but your own!'

'What do you mean?'

'How do you think I felt when I met that train and you weren't on it?' he demanded grimly.

Joanna was taken aback. 'I—well, I didn't know you would meet the train,' she protested.

'But you were aware that you would be expected to be on it?'

'I—suppose so. But Brad said he could have me here before the train, and I thought——'

'Yes? What did you think?'

Joanna hunched her shoulders. 'All right, I'm sorry. Perhaps I should have come by train. But after my—*welcome* last time, I didn't suppose my non-appearance would arouse too much disappointment.'

Shannon's expression frightened her. 'Why, you——' He bit off an epithet. 'You deserve hanging for that remark! My God, have you any idea of the risk you run just being here? A lone woman—a lone *white* woman in a predominantly black community? Your father was crazy allowing you to come here, but that's typical of him! So long as he gets what he wants, he doesn't care who gets hurt along the way!'

'Oh, Shannon——'

'When I found that you'd gone back to Menawi——'

'But you told me to go!'

'Not unescorted. I was going to take you myself—make sure you got safely on the plane.'

'But you were ill!'

'Precisely. And thanks to you and Camilla, I had no choice in the matter.'

'Shannon, I was all right.'

'There are men in Menawi, Joanna, unscrupulous men, who would pay dearly to have possession of a girl with your —attributes. Do you take my meaning?'

Joanna gasped. 'I don't believe that sort of thing still goes on!'

'Let me assure you, it does.' Shannon's eyes were hard. 'These people respect their own kind, but they have no respect for white women, who go around half naked most of the time!'

'But—but I don't!'

Shannon raked a hand through his hair. 'God, Joanna, I don't need a crystal ball to know you're wearing next to nothing under that shirt and jeans.'

Joanna's face burned. 'Oh—oh, very well. I take your

point.'

'That's good. So now perhaps you have some small idea of my feelings when you didn't appear off that train!' He uttered a savage oath. 'You asked about my attitude towards Steiner, didn't you? My God, I didn't speak to him, Joanna, because if I had, I think I would have wrung his neck!'

'Oh, Shannon.' Joanna felt ashamed. 'I really didn't think you'd worry.'

'No ... well ...' Shannon ran a hand round the back of his neck, lifting his damp shirt away from his skin. 'At least you're here now and unharmed.' He paused. 'Did you spend the weekend with Steiner?'

Joanna dropped her bag down on to a chair. 'I spent yesterday with him,' she admitted reluctantly. Then she looked at him again. 'I didn't know there were no trains on Sundays, and no one bothered to enlighten me.'

Shannon studied her flushed face. 'No doubt he proved an entertaining escort,' he commented tersely.

'He's pleasant,' Joanna agreed, wishing Shannon would stop looking at her as if he disliked her. 'And if what you say is true, perhaps it's just as well he was around. At least I wasn't alone.'

'Mmm.' Shannon sounded unconvinced.

'Shannon, he knows I'm engaged!' she exclaimed, needing somehow to defend herself. 'He saw my ring, just as you did.' She shook her head. 'Anyway, as you say, I'm here now. And if you expected me back, why did you let Jacob dismantle the bed?'

'The bed's in the study,' Shannon retorted levelly. 'I shall be using it tonight.'

'You will?' Joanna's lips parted in dismay as she realised she had not even asked him how he was feeling. 'There's no need for you to——'

'Don't talk nonsense!' Shannon sounded bored by the whole affair. 'When are you planning to return to England?'

64

Joanna shrugged her slim shoulders. 'I—haven't thought about it. At least, not in detail.'

'Then I suggest we leave the day after tomorrow,' said Shannon thoughtfully. 'That gives me the rest of today and all tomorrow to get things organised here.'

Joanna could feel her facial muscles stiffening. So no matter how concerned he had been about her, he was still determined that she should leave as soon as possible. She despised herself for feeling so desolated by the knowledge. This place wasn't good for her. Perhaps it was as well she was being given no choice in the matter.

Taking a deep breath, she exclaimed: 'There's no need for you to organise anything. Apart from the fact that you've scarcely recovered from that illness, I've already made the trip twice on my own. There's no reason why I shouldn't reach the airport without mishap. I can take a taxi from the station, if that will ease your mind. Just leave me to make my own arrangements.'

'No.' Shannon's denial brooked no argument.

'Why? *Why?*' Joanna was trembling, but she couldn't help it. 'Are—are you afraid I might overstay my welcome if the decision is left to me?' she choked.

'You should know you couldn't do that!' he told her grimly, taking a step forward and then checking himself as she swayed towards him. 'No,' he muttered. 'No, Joanna.' He turned away, and it was all she could do to prevent herself from going to him and pressing her face against his back. 'But,' he added slowly, as though the words were drawn from him against his will, 'if I'm coming to England, and I must be crazy even to consider it, I have to make certain arrangements.'

Joanna's heart was pounding so loudly, she thought it must be audible even to him. 'You—you're coming to—England?' she echoed disbelievingly.

'That was what you wanted, wasn't it?' He was looking at her out of the corners of his eyes.

'Oh, I—well, yes. Yes. You know it is, but——'

'Don't get carried away. I'm coming to speak to your father, that's all,' he said flatly. 'I've realised I don't have the kind of conscience that permits me to dismiss the request of a dying man out of hand. But don't expect me to stay, Joanna. Don't expect that!'

CHAPTER FIVE

THE powerful Boeing made its scheduled landing at Nairobi in the late afternoon. Passengers were politely informed that they might leave the aircraft, but not the airport, and be prepared for their flight to be recalled in one hour. Joanna had her first taste of the milder Kenyan climate as she descended the two flights of steps from the aircraft to the tarmac, and after the humidity of Kwyana, Nairobi's eighty degrees struck her as comparatively cool, particularly as there was a refreshing breeze blowing down from the mountains.

As they walked towards the airport buildings, Joanna stole a glance at Shannon. In a navy denim suit, the jacket slung carelessly over his shoulder, his cream silk shirt accentuating his tan, he had attracted a number of interested stares from the other female passengers. Joanna guessed there was some speculation about their relationship, and as she was wearing a ring, they probably thought she was his fiancée. She wondered at the pang this thought aroused in her.

The airport itself was much the same as any other international airport, and after clearing passport control, Shannon guided her towards the airport bar. At this late hour of the afternoon, most of the other passengers had the same idea, and there was quite a press of people waiting for service. But Shannon managed to get two lagers and brought them over to the corner table where Joanna had secured two stools. The lager was cold and sharp and caught the back of her throat, and she choked on the first mouthful so that Shannon had to thump her on the back to help her regain her breath.

'You enjoyed that, didn't you?' she accused him through watering eyes, when she had regained her breath. 'You didn't have to hit me so hard!'

'I'm sorry.' Shannon offered a reluctant apology, but amusement lurked around his mouth.

'I don't believe you are,' she retorted, aware that they had attracted the attention of two American girls who were travelling on the same flight, and who had been giving Shannon an intent appraisal. 'I think I'd rather have choked!'

Shannon shook his head patiently. 'Now I don't believe that,' he told her, his eyes on hers. 'What would—Philip? That was his name, wasn't it? Yes. What would Philip have to say if I allowed his fiancée to expire in a glass of lager at Nairobi airport?'

Joanna looked down into her glass. She knew he was only teasing her, that since leaving Kwyana he had made a definite effort to behave towards her as he would towards a younger sister, but she didn't want to talk about Philip now. Her time alone with Shannon was rapidly dwindling away, and she knew that once they reached her father's house it would be almost impossible for them to have a private conversation.

'Shannon,' she ventured huskily, 'Shannon, what will you do?'

But Shannon didn't answer her. Indeed, she doubted if he had even heard her above the constant buzz of conversation all around them. One of the American girls had leant across to speak to him on some pretext of asking the time, and was not wasting the opportunity. She offered Shannon one of her long American cigarettes, and although Shannon rarely smoked, he accepted one, steadying her hand as she held out the flame of her lighter.

The feeling which swept over Joanna as she watched them rocked her to the core of her being, and her nails curled painfully into her palms. The realisation that she was *jealous* made her reach unsteadily for the lager, downing the lot in an effort to ease the sudden constriction in her throat.

'Are you trying to out-drink me?'

Shannon's lazy mockery was more than she could bear. With a mumbled apology she got to her feet, and ignoring his puzzled stare, walked quickly away to the ladies' room.

There was a queue, the same as at the bar, but Joanna joined it, not really needing the loo, but glad of any excuse to avoid listening to Shannon laughing with the American girl.

'Say, is this the end of the line?'

For a moment Joanna thought the girl had followed her, but when she turned she found it was the second American who was standing right behind her.

'I—I think so,' she answered shortly, and swung round again, but the American was not prepared to be dismissed so easily.

'You have to line up for everything these days, don't you?' she went on easily. 'I guess we're turning into a conveyor belt society, all waiting in line for something.' She laughed, when Joanna didn't, and then said: 'Have you been on holiday in Menawi?'

Joanna sighed, but it was not in her nature to be rude, and she couldn't go on ignoring the other girl. 'I—sort of,' she conceded, hoping that would satisfy her. 'Have you?'

'Actually, my friend and I are doing cultural studies,' the girl explained confidentially. 'We've been visiting various parts of Africa studying life styles and customs. It's surprising how fascinating we found it all.'

'I see.'

'Yes. I mean, Africans are amazingly artistic people. Well, look at their music! But one doesn't always associate their culture with beauty, and yet some of their weapons and utensils have been compared to the Romanesque period of European history.' She paused. 'Of course, some of their customs are not so appealing, but overall we were impressed,

I can tell you.'

'How interesting.'

Joanna took another step forward in the queue, wondering how much longer they were going to have to wait. Distracting as the American girl's narrative might be, she was finding herself growing perversely impatient to get back to Shannon again.

'For instance . . .' Joanna closed her eyes as the girl began again: 'Some tribes can actually justify cannibalism as an excuse for not starving. Naturally, they don't just eat their next-door neighbour, or anything like that, but the warriors killed in tribal battles provide food for their tables. Oh, well,' she laughed, 'I don't suppose they actually have tables, but you know what I mean.'

Joanna forced a smile.

'There are some customs common to most of the tribes— like the bride price, for example. I expect you've heard of that. After all, it was common enough in England once, wasn't it? I mean—girls had to have dowries, that sort of thing?' She waited for Joanna's silent acknowledgement. 'Fortunately, we modern girls don't have to cope with that! How terrible to wonder if a man was only marrying you for what you could give him!'

'I imagine it still happens,' remarked Joanna dryly, and aroused a titter of derision from her companion.

'Do you think so?' Her eyes narrowed. 'But I don't suppose your fiancé chose you for those reasons, did he?' She pulled her lower lip between her teeth. 'You—er—you don't have to mind Lou Ellen, by the way. She can't resist an attractive male, and your fiancé's certainly that!'

'He's not my fiancé!' stated Joanna flatly. How could she pretend that he was, attractive though that idea might be, when Shannon was most likely explaining their relationship to this girl's friend?

'He's not?' There was obvious surprise now.

'No. He—he's my half-brother.'

70

'Half-brother!' echoed the girl. 'Well! For brother and sister you sure look different, him so dark and you so fair.'

'We had different mothers,' explained Joanna shortly.

'Oh, I see. And they were a blonde and a brunette.'

'No. That is—I don't know.' Joanna felt a frown crease her brow. All the pictures she had seen of Shannon's mother had shown her to be a woman as fair as, if not fairer than Joanna's own mother. And their father's grey hair had once been auburn. Shannon must be a throwback to his grand-parents, she thought impatiently, and she had no idea what colouring they had been.

To her relief, she was next in line, and when she emerged from the cubicle the other girl was not around. She rinsed her face and hands, ran a comb through her hair, and left the cloakroom before she appeared.

Shannon wasn't at their table when she got back, how-ever, and she was looking round in alarm when the girl called Lou Ellen said: 'He's at the bar, honey. He won't be long.'

Joanna smiled her thanks, and seated herself with some reluctance. If Lou Ellen was as adept at conducting a con-versation as her friend, she would rather face the heat out-side. But apparently Lou Ellen's charms were reserved for the opposite sex, and apart from exchanging a sympathetic look now and then, she didn't say anything.

The heat in the bar was quite intense, in spite of the air-conditioning. The smoke from cigarettes and cigars thick-ened the air, and Joanna was glad she had chosen to travel in a halter-necked shirt and a plain denim skirt which left her midriff bare. Even so, the back of her neck was damp, and her thighs stuck to the chair where they touched.

Shannon came back carrying a tray on which resided four frosted glasses, each decorated with slices of citrus fruit and sprigs of mint. Joanna didn't need to be a mind-reader to guess who the two other glasses were for, and she didn't re-spond to the smile Shannon cast inquiringly in her direction

71

as he took his seat.

'You took your time,' he observed in an undertone, after Lou Ellen had thanked him for the highball she was tasting.

'There was a queue,' retorted Joanna, with some asperity. Then: 'Why on earth did you get me this? I prefer lager.'

Shannon removed the offending glass from her fingers with controlled violence, and set it down beside his own. Then before she could stop him, he was on his way to the bar again. Lou Ellen quirked a mocking eyebrow, but as she must have heard what Joanna had said, she made no comment.

Shannon returned a few minutes later with the lager Joanna had requested, and she accepted it from him rather ungracefully, saying: 'Thanks,' in a small voice.

The stewardess's voice over the tannoy system distracted Shannon's attention, and Joanna stiffened when she heard the number of their flight. Unfortunately, it appeared that the 747 had developed a fault after landing, and it was expected that take-off would be delayed for a further two hours. The airline suggested that passengers should take dinner in the restaurant at their expense, and a further delay was not anticipated.

'Well, at least I don't have to swallow these in five minutes,' remarked Shannon, smiling at Lou Ellen, and she laughingly conceded his point.

'You'd probably take off without the plane,' she joked, and Joanna felt completely superfluous.

The other American girl chose that moment to return from the ladies' room, looking anxious until she saw her friend. 'Was that our flight I heard called?'

'No such luck, Susie,' responded Lou Ellen, shaking her head. 'Here,' she pushed the other highball towards her, 'Shannon bought that for you.'

Shannon! Joanna's fists clenched in her lap. That hadn't taken long.

'What's going on?' The girl Lou Ellen had addressed as Susie sat down and looked questioningly from one to another of them. She raised her glass to Shannon. 'I could have sworn I heard the number of our flight.'

'You did,' said Shannon, joining her in raising his glass. 'The plane's developed a fault. Two hours' delay.'

'Oh, no!' Susie's eyes rolled heavenward.

'It could be worse,' remarked Lou Ellen practically. 'We might have taken off before the fault was discovered.'

'Say, that's right.' Susie nodded her agreement, and Lou Ellen went on:

'Besides, it's not so bad here. And the company's good.' Her eyes twinkled at Shannon.

Joanna turned her head and stared determinedly out of the windows. The short sub-tropical twilight was beginning to cast shadows that had not been there half an hour ago, and soon it would be dark. She wondered with a tightening of her lips whether Shannon would invite the two American girls to join them for dinner. It was not unlikely, and she wished she did not feel this intense antipathy towards them. Why couldn't she talk to them as Shannon was doing, be friendly—behave as Shannon's sister ought to behave?

Shannon had finished his first highball and had started on his second when she looked back at the others. She encountered his scornful gaze and immediately wished the floor would open up and swallow her. Why had she behaved so childishly over the drinks, just because he was making casual conversation with a fellow traveller? She deserved his contempt.

'When you've finished that, can we go and have something to eat?' she suggested in a low voice.

Shannon set down his glass. 'If you're hungry,' he conceded.

'Aren't you?'

'Not particularly.'

Joanna sighed: 'Perhaps—perhaps Lou Ellen and Susie

73

might like to join us,' she ventured, and Shannon's eyes narrowed impatiently.

'Do you want me to ask them?' he inquired, with cold detachment, and Joanna made an uncertain movement of her shoulders.

'That's up to you.'

'How about us all having dinner together?'

Lou Ellen's drawling tones interrupted them, and Shannon's lips twisted wryly before he turned to the American and said: 'Why not? It will help to pass the time.'

'That's some line you've got there,' remarked Lou Ellen, assuming a wounded air. 'You really know how to make a girl feel wanted.'

The restaurant was over-worked, but they eventually were shown to a table and a reasonable meal was served. During the meal, Susie began asking Shannon about his work, and Joanna learned more about gold and gold mining in those few minutes than she had learned in the time she was in Kwyana.

'Do they hand out samples?' Lou Ellen laughed, after Shannon had astonished them all by telling them that a single grain of gold could be beaten to cover an area of seventy-five square inches. 'I expect it's a terrible temptation to the men.'

'You'd need a truck to steal enough gold to make it even half worthwhile,' he answered. 'Lode gold, that's the kind we're mining, is part of solid rock, in our case quartz. We mine tons of the stuff, and the gold is usually found in small veins scattered through the rock. The real difficulty is separating the gold from the quartz.'

'But isn't it dangerous working below ground?' exclaimed Susie.

'All mining involves an element of danger,' Shannon agreed, leaning back in his chair. 'My job is to ensure that that element is kept to the minimum.'

'Do you go underground?' asked Lou Ellen.

'If there's trouble, it's my job to locate it, and formulate the best method of dealing with it. The underground manager——'

'So you only go underground when it's most dangerous to do so?' cried Joanna, in dismay, and then coloured when they all turned to look at her.

'The safety of the men is my concern,' stated Shannon levelly. 'It's my job. If we get a pressure burst, if there's flooding or fire, it's up to me to see that the men get out alive.'

Joanna couldn't eat any more. Pushing back her chair, she got to her feet and walked quickly out of the restaurant. She didn't care that she hadn't excused herself, that this was twice she had walked out on him; she simply couldn't bear to sit there any longer and listen to Lou Ellen and Susie applauding his courage. She felt physically sick, and not even the knowledge that he was coming to England could shift the devastating realisation that so long as Shannon was employed by the Lushasan Mining Authority he ran the risk of losing his life in some dark cavern thousands of feet below the earth.

Shannon eventually found her in the dimly-lit departure lounge, huddled in solitary isolation in one corner. The lounge was noisy with the sounds of frustrated children, babies crying, and transistor radios blaring out the latest pop tunes. Delayed passengers sprawled beside their hand luggage, reading newspapers or grumbling about the lack of amenities. He came strolling towards her, stepping over legs and handbags, children's improvised games, his jacket hanging from one hand, the other pushed lazily into his pocket. He hesitated a moment, but when she refused to give him more than a cursory glance, he came down on the seat beside her, his wine-scented breath fanning her neck.

'You're crazy, do you know that?' he muttered huskily. 'I've been looking everywhere for you!'

'I'm sorry.'

75

Her response was mechanical, and she heard his muffled oath. 'Why the devil did you walk out of the restaurant like that? What did I say? For God's sake, Joanna, you must have known that mining for gold was no picnic!'

Joanna turned indignant eyes upon him. 'I don't suppose I thought about it in those terms,' she retorted, through trembling lips.

'So now you have. What of it? All jobs contain some risk. Good God, I could—turn a tractor over and kill myself tomorrow. You don't think about things like that. You just do your job and hope for the best.'

'But you don't have to work in mining!' she cried. 'You need never go back to Kwyana. The estate's yours. Your father said so.'

'*Your* father, Joanna!' he stated coldly. 'Not mine.'

'That's crazy, Shannon! Of course he's your father, too. You can't shrug off the relationship of a lifetime!'

Shannon dropped his coat over the back of a chair. 'You don't understand, Joanna. You never have. But make no mistake—this is a visit, nothing more. I shall not be staying in England.'

She hunched her shoulders, withdrawing as far from him as it was physically possible. He didn't care that his safety might mean something to her, to *all* of them. How could he deny his own father with such callous unconcern? He was right, she didn't understand.

'Oh, *Joanna*!' He was looking down at her, and the words seemed torn from him. She felt his fingers curling round the bare skin of her upper arm, warm hard fingers that touched her with lingering possession. Then he bent his head, and her shoulder lifted involuntarily to meet the lips that sought her creamy flesh. 'You should stop me, Joanna.'

She half turned to look at him, her breath catching in her throat at the look in his eyes.

'Don't—look at me—like that!' she whispered, but it was already too late. His firm mouth was parting her lips

76

with an urgency that sent the blood hammering through her veins, throbbing through her head, until all coherent thought ceased. He smelt so warm and male, and her hands slid up to the back of his neck, twining in the hair that grew there, holding him closer. His splayed fingers were at her midriff, bare between the halter top and her skirt, arching her against him, and she could feel his heart pounding against her breasts.

The flight call seemed to bring him to his senses. With a groan of protest, he thrust her away from him, getting to his feet and reaching for his jacket. He buttoned his shirt with fingers that were not quite steady about their task, and thrust it impatiently back into the waistband of his pants.

Joanna remained where he had left her. She, too, was shaken and trembling, and she wondered where she was going to find the energy to walk the distance to the plane. She did not dare to examine the consequences of what had just happened, but she could not believe that the way she was feeling was wrong. From the moment they had met she had been aware of him in a way no girl should be aware of her half-brother, and what had just happened was a culmination of that attraction.

The look on Shannon's face was not encouraging. His mouth which only a few moments ago had been sensually demanding on hers, was drawn into a grim line, and there was impatience in the way he said: 'Stop looking like that, Joanna. We haven't done anything morally wrong, if that's what's troubling you. Except perhaps to—Philip. I'm sorry, but he needn't ever know, need he? Just forget it!'

'Forget it?'

Her tormented cry was drowned beneath a repetition of the flight call, and she was forced to grab her belongings and follow Shannon towards the group moving steadily in the direction of the departure gate. Lou Ellen and Susie had rejoined them, and their apparently sincere queries as to why Joanna had so suddenly left the restaurant earlier filled the awkward moments. But everything Shannon had said, everything they had done, filled her brain with jumbled confusion, and the reality of her coming marriage to Philip had never seemed more remote.

If she had expected Shannon to talk to her once they were aboard the plane, she was mistaken. He settled himself in his seat and then closed his eyes, pointedly ignoring her. Joanna stared blindly through the darkened window as the plane took off, pretending an interest in the mass of lights below them, while she acknowledged the realisation that so far as Shannon was concerned she knew practically nothing about him.

CHAPTER SIX

THE Boeing landed at Heathrow in the early hours of the morning, London time. Shannon had slept for most of the long flight, and seemed physically relaxed. But Joanna had only succeeded in dozing, and the sight of the steadily falling February rain was sufficient to depress her utterly. Shannon himself was cool and detached, and she found it difficult to ally him with the man who had held her in his arms and kissed her with such passion the evening before. But perhaps that was his intention. The incident at Nairobi airport had been a moment out of time, never to be repeated.

They cleared passport control, collected their suitcases on a trolley, and walked through Customs. Formalities were kept to a minimum, and within three-quarters of an hour of landing they emerged from the international terminal buildings to find a taxi.

'I suggest we go to a hotel, and try and get some sleep for the rest of the night,' suggested Shannon thoughtfully, noticing the dark rings around Joanna's green eyes.

'I'm not tired,' she denied, drawing her sheepskin jacket closer about her, glad she had not packed it as she had been tempted to do in the heat of Menawi. 'I'd rather go straight to the station. There may be a train to Carlisle around six.'

Shannon's lips thinned. 'Nevertheless, we will go to a hotel,' he stated flatly, and Joanna pursed her lips as she climbed unaided into the back of the cab.

They drove to the St Mark's hotel, which was near Euston station, and the night porter arranged for them to have two adjoining single rooms on the fourth floor. Joanna refused to look at Shannon as they went up in the lift, but

79

he seemed immune to her defiance. When they reached her door, he unlocked it and carried her cases inside for her.

'Well, this should be all right,' he commented, looking about him critically at the beige and brown curtains and matching bedspread. He tossed her key on to the bed, and walked towards the door. 'Get some sleep. You look exhausted. We needn't hurry this morning. We can always catch an afternoon train.' He paused. 'I'll just be next door if you need me.'

Joanna's resistance ebbed away. 'Stay with me, Shannon!' she breathed, and his tawny eyes darkened to burnished amber. She looked a little lost and alone, standing there in the middle of the floor and she saw his fists clench involuntarily.

Then with a muffled oath, he walked through the open doorway, saying: 'Go to sleep, Joanna!' before it slammed heavily behind him.

Wearily, Joanna took off her clothes, and slipped naked between the sheets. The bed was cold, but she didn't notice it. She was cold already, and it was not a physical discomfort.

The sound of the traffic awoke her, and she lay for some time trying to get her bearings. Then the memory of all that had gone before came back to her, and she rolled miserably on to her stomach, burying her face in the pillow.

Eventually she aroused herself sufficiently to look at her watch and was startled to find it was after eleven o'clock. The room seemed absurdly dull for that time of day, but when she rolled out of bed and padded to the window, she found that it was sleeting and everywhere looked grey and depressing.

She showered in her bathroom, and then opened one of her suitcases and took out the maroon jersey slack suit she had worn to travel out to South Africa. It was more suitable to the weather than the thin summer clothes she had been wearing, and complemented the extreme fairness of her hair.

There were no sounds from Shannon's room, but she went and knocked at his door. This elicited no response, and with a frown she collected her handbag and went downstairs. The receptionist politely informed her that Mr Carne had gone out over an hour ago, but had left a message that she should have some brunch and wait for him.

Joanna decided to do as he suggested, but only ordered toast and coffee instead of the grill the waiter suggested. She was drinking her second cup when Shannon appeared in the doorway, dark and attractive in a dark brown suede suit, and a toning cinnamon-coloured shirt. His tie was brown, too, and Joanna thought he had never looked more sexually disturbing. He came lazily across to her table, the restaurant was practically deserted at this hour of the morning, and lounged into the seat opposite. He surveyed her appearance with casual appraisal, and then said quietly: 'You look better. I gather you got some sleep.'

Joanna's cup clattered into its saucer. 'Yes. Thank you.' She moved her shoulders awkwardly. 'Where have you been?'

'Renewing my acquaintance with London—buying myself a coat.' He shrugged. 'I went up to my room when I got back. I thought you might still be asleep. When I could get no reply from your room, I came down here.'

Joanna nodded. 'I—would you like some coffee? Have you had any breakfast?'

'I had something earlier,' he answered. 'And no, thanks. I'm going to have a beer in a few minutes. I've made inquiries about trains and there's one at twelve-fifty-five. I suggest we get that, and have lunch on the train.'

Joanna nodded her agreement. 'All right.'

Shannon leant towards her suddenly, his eyes intent. 'Are you all right, though?' he demanded impatiently. 'God, you still look—drained! I'm sorry, Joanna. I'm sorry for what happened. I blame myself entirely. I shouldn't have touched you. But I couldn't help myself. That's no excuse

81

I know, but—well, you make me——' He broke off, and leaned back again, faint colour darkening his tan. 'It won't happen again, I promise you.' He felt around in his pockets and produced a pack of cigarettes, taking one out and putting it between his lips. 'You'd better tell me about—Philip. It wouldn't do for me to meet him not knowing a single thing about him except his name and where he lives. Everyone will be expecting you to have told me all about him.'

'Do you *really* want to know about Philip?' she exclaimed in a choked voice, and her words checked him as he was applying his lighter flame to his cigarette.

'No,' he told her honestly. 'I already dislike him intensely. But I think you'd better tell me just the same.'

Joanna rested an elbow on the table, supporting her head with her hand. 'I—I don't want to talk about Philip, Shannon.'

Shannon inhaled deeply on his cigarette, his eyes narrowing. 'You love him, don't you?'

'What? Oh, yes, *yes*. Of course I love him. He—he's a wonderful man. I—I just don't feel like talking about him now.'

'Why not?'

She lifted bruised eyes to meet his. 'You know why.'

Shannon got abruptly to his feet. 'I need that beer,' he said harshly, and strode out of the restaurant.

The train arrived at Carlisle just before five o'clock. The weather had not improved, and it was much colder here than in London. Because the train had been full, they had been separated for most of the journey, and Shannon, Joanna knew, had spent a lot of his time in the buffet. She guessed he needed a drink before facing his father again, and she wished alcohol could provide some release for her. But the only time she had ever drunk too much, at a party, she had been violently sick afterwards, and she did not want that to happen now.

As they passed through the ticket barrier, she said: 'Shall I telephone Philip? He could come and pick us up. There isn't a bus until six o'clock.'

Shannon shook his head grimly, and glancing round summoned the nearest cab. 'I'm not waiting around for anyone in this!' he declared, handing their luggage to the driver who stowed it in the boot. 'Go on, get in. I'll sit in front.'

Joanna climbed obediently into the back of the musty-smelling cab, closing the door behind her, and drawing her legs closely together. The last lap, she thought bitterly, and he would not even sit beside her.

It was too dark to distinguish any landmarks once the lights of the town were left behind. Just beyond Thursby, they turned off the main Carlisle to Cockermouth road, taking the narrower, winding track which led along the banks of the River Mallow, to Mallowsdale. The Hall, which had been the home of the Carne family for generations, stood about a mile from the village, and as the road twisted and turned between snow-capped hedges, Joanna could see the lights of the house gleaming through the bare twigs. She wondered what Shannon's feelings must be, coming home after all these years, but he was talking desultorily to the taxi driver, and seemed unmoved by the poignancy of the situation. She refused to consider what his coming home had meant to her ...

The taxi turned between the stone posts which flanked the driveway to the house. Wooden gates stood wide as always, but as they neared the building, her father's collie, Bess, set up a wild barking.

'Seems like someone knows you're here,' remarked the taxi driver, with a grin at Shannon. 'Your dog, is he?'

Shannon shook his head, casting a faintly derisive glance in Joanna's direction. 'No,' he said briefly. 'Not mine.'

The front door had opened by the time the taxi reached the house, but it was not any member of the Carne family who closed it behind him and came slowly down the steps. It was Philip Lawson, and as the vehicle's headlights swept the area in front of the house, Joanna could see Philip's Triumph parked a few yards from the house. He had halted, obviously as surprised by their arrival as Joanna found she was to see him, and he shaded his eyes against the headlights' glare and waited until the taxi came to a halt.

Without waiting for anyone's assistance, Joanna thrust open her door and climbed out. All of a sudden she needed Philip, and she was reassured by his instantaneous reaction. 'Joanna!' he exclaimed, half disbelievingly. 'Oh, Joanna!' He came towards her, pulling her eagerly into his arms. 'I never expected it to be you! I only got a letter from you this morning telling me you were going to spend a few days in Kwyana.' He raised his head after giving her a welcoming hug. 'Where's Shannon? Is he with you?'

'Yes ...' Joanna's response was stiff, but she couldn't help it. She had been aware of Shannon getting out of the car behind them, of his brief exchange with the driver, and after settling the fare getting their cases out of the boot. But now she was forced to turn to him as the taxi reversed cautiously away, and she was glad of the sheltering darkness to hide her flushed cheeks. 'Come and meet my fiancé, Shannon,' she said jerkily. 'Philip—this is my—this is Shannon.'

The two men shook hands, Philip following this up with his usual friendly greeting: 'Glad to know you, Shannon. I know your father's going to be pleased to see you.'

There was stiffness between the two men, and Joanna could not help but be aware of it. The sleet was turning to snow, and in the half light she saw the tightness in Shannon's face, his eyes narrowing as he looked up at the house. But his tone was civil as he thanked Philip for his welcome, adding: 'The place doesn't change much, does it? I don't know why I thought it would.'

'You'd better come along inside,' exclaimed Philip, urging them both up the steps to the door, but Joanna hung back, trying to see her home through Shannon's eyes. He was right, of course, it didn't change. But that was one of the things she most loved about it.

Mallowsdale Hall was not a large country house, but it was built of stone, and stone was built to last. It stood on a slight rise, backed by a copse of fir trees, the ground sloping away beyond to the banks of the Mallow. Long, mullioned windows looked proudly over land which had been in the Carne family for almost two hundred years, good grazing land, without the gentleness to be found further south. The first Carnes had been mine-owners, using the estate as a country retreat, but gradually, as standards of living levelled out, they had been forced into becoming farmers themselves. Over the years, the estate had dwindled in size. Land taxes and death duties had meant the sale of much of the property, and the Hall, the land immediately surrounding it, and the home farm, were all that was left of the original estate. Still, there was always plenty to be done, and since her father's stroke, Philip had spent more and more time at Mallowsdale.

'Joanna!'

Philip's slightly impatient summons interrupted her reverie, and realising the two men were waiting for her, she hurried after them. It was Shannon who opened the door, however, Shannon who entered the house first; Shannon— his face contemptuous of his presence here as the prodigal returned.

Jessie Duxbury, the Carnes' daily, was crossing the hall with a tray, on which reposed a single glass and a bottle of Scotch, when the door opened, and she turned with a start to face them. Then her homely face cleared as she recognised the boy she had first seen when he was only a few hours old.

'Shannon!' she exclaimed, her eyes filling with tears. 'Eh, Shannon, you've come home!'

85

Shannon's expression lost its bitterness for a moment, and he went to bend and kiss Jessie's lined cheek. 'Now then, Jessie,' he greeted her gently. 'You don't look a day older than when I went away.'

Jessie struggled to hold back her tears. 'You're a rare one to talk—going away like that. Not caring what happened to us all!'

'That's not true, Jessie. Of course, I cared. But a man has to be—independent.'

'You were ever that,' muttered Jessie, brushing an impatient hand across her eyes. 'I heard the dog barking. Bess knows when there's something up.'

Another woman appeared, attracted no doubt by the unexpected sound of voices. Smaller than her daughter, still with that touching air of helplessness which had first aroused Maxwell Carne's protective instincts, Catherine Carne stared at the gathering in the hall with faintly disbelieving eyes. Her gaze moved quickly from her daughter to Philip to Shannon, and then back to her daughter again as she moved forward.

'Joanna! Why didn't you let us know you were coming?'

Joanna allowed her mother to give her a swift embrace, and then said: 'We didn't know, Mummy, honestly. It all happened so suddenly.' She glanced awkwardly at Shannon. 'I cabled you that—that Shannon was ill, and as soon as he was better . . .'

'. . . we came,' finished Shannon dryly. 'Hello, Mother, it's good to see you.'

Catherine hesitated only a moment, before embracing her stepson, and like Jessie she was visibly moved when she drew back. 'It's good to see you, too, Shannon,' she echoed his words. 'Did you have a good journey?'

'Apart from a couple of hours' delay in Nairobi, it was reasonable,' answered Shannon, and Joanna envied him his apparent coolness and detachment. 'It's cold here, though, isn't it? I guess my blood's thinned over the years.'

'And no wonder, in that heathen place!' put in Jessie reprovingly. Then she nodded at the tray in her hand, seeking Catherine's advice. 'Do I take this in? He'll be wondering what's going on.'

Catherine looked flustered for a moment. 'Oh—oh, yes, I suppose——'

'Kate! *Kate*! Jessie! In God's name, where are you, woman?'

They all stiffened at the sound of that harsh, commanding voice, even Philip, but Joanna's eyes were drawn to Shannon yet again. He had stiffened, too, but there was a line of grim determination around his mouth, and without asking permission he took the tray from Jessie's unresisting hands.

'I'll take that,' he said, uncompromisingly, and they all watched as he crossed the square, polished wood blocks of the hall and rapped loudly at the library door before letting himself inside.

The silence was unnerving. They were all straining their ears to hear the first words of that long-awaited confrontation, and Joanna suddenly couldn't stand it any more.

'Is there anything to eat, Mummy?' she asked, in a high, unnatural voice, even though food was the last thing she was needing right now. 'I haven't had a thing since lunchtime.'

Her words seemed to animate all of them at once. Jessie bustled off to the kitchen, her mother visibly gathered herself, and Philip slung a casual arm about her shoulders.

'Look, I've got to go,' he said regretfully. 'Mother's got a meal waiting for me. I wish you could join us, but I suppose you'd rather spend the evening with your parents and Shannon.'

Joanna hesitated. Quite honestly, the idea of getting into Philip's car and driving away with him appealed tremendously, but her mother's expression was sufficient to convince her that she could not do that. Instead, she compromised.

'Why don't you come over later on, Philip?' she invited, knowing full well he would not refuse.

'I suppose I could.' Philip looked at Mrs Carne.

Catherine shook her head bewilderedly. 'Of course, Philip. Do what you want. You're almost one of the family. I don't know how we would have managed without your help these past weeks. You're always welcome at Mallowsdale.'

Philip's face flushed with pleasure, and Joanna wondered why she didn't feel more enthusiasm in this knowledge.

'It's kind of you to say so, Mrs Carne,' Philip was saying now. 'I always feel—at home here.'

Catherine made a deprecating gesture. 'I'll be in the kitchen when you want me, Joanna,' she said, anticipating their desire to be alone, and left them.

Philip's eyes were tender as he looked down at his fiancée, his fingers seeking his ring on her left hand, pressing it insinuatively. 'I've missed you, Joanna,' he murmured huskily, and she tried to respond as she knew he expected. But when he lifted his head she could tell from his expression she had not entirely succeeded. 'What is it?' he asked, his brows drawing together. 'What's wrong? Did *he* give you a hard time?'

They both knew what he was talking about, but Joanna didn't want to talk about Shannon. 'I'm tired, Philip,' she exclaimed defensively, despising herself for feeling this way. 'How—how's Daddy? I forgot to ask.'

Philip shrugged. 'You heard, didn't you? He's just as—irascible as ever. Perhaps he'll calm down now that his son has returned. If he doesn't take care, he'll kill himself as well as the fatted calf!'

There was a trace of bitterness in Philip's voice, but Joanna scarcely registered it. She cast anxious eyes towards the closed library door. From beyond the heavy panels, the low murmur of voices could be heard, but the thickness of the walls disguised the tenor of the words being spoken.

'Is he going to stay?' Philip was speaking again, and Joanna forced herself to concentrate on what he was saying. 'Shannon? Is he going to take over?'

She felt ill-equipped to answer him, to put up any arguments for or against right now. But she had to be honest. 'I—I don't think so,' she admitted reluctantly. 'I really don't think so.'

'You don't?' Philip's expression was suddenly very hard to read. 'Why not? Is he going back to Africa?' Her face revealed her fears that this was so, and he turned away from her, clenching his fists. 'Doesn't he care about the estate?' he demanded harshly. 'That Mallowsdale is his home? His inheritance? My God, your father's made that abundantly clear, hasn't he?'

Just for a moment Joanna heard the note of resentment in Philip's angry tones, and wondered whether he had, at any time, entertained the idea that she might inherit the estate. After all, when he and his parents had first come to live at High Stoop, it had been natural for them to suppose that she was an only child. Her father had not talked about Shannon in those days, his name had rarely if ever been mentioned. But once Joanna started going out with Philip she had explained the situation, and he had not seemed affected by the news.

Even so, it was not until her father had had his stroke that he had become so fanatical that Shannon should come home. Then, it had seemed the only thing that kept him alive through those dangerous early days when the doctors had given him a less than evens chance of survival.

Now, Joanna thrust these traitorous thoughts aside. Philip's fears, his anxieties, were all for her father. He knew, better than anyone, that Maxwell Carne would never farm his estate again. And if Shannon didn't take over, who would?

'Perhaps we should wait and see,' she ventured now, and Philip swung round again, controlling the anger he had so unexpectedly displayed.

'Perhaps we should,' he agreed with a sigh. 'And I must go. I promised I'd be home for the evening meal half an hour ago. But when Mother hears that you're home again, she'll forgive me.'

Joanna forced a smile. 'Give her my love.'

'I will. I know she's looking forward to seeing you. She's found a sewing pattern which she's convinced will be ideal for your wedding dress.'

Joanna caught back the sigh that almost escaped her. 'I—I'll look forward to seeing it.'

'And I'll see you later.'

'Oh, yes—yes, later.' Joanna wished she sounded more enthusiastic. It wasn't fair to make Philip the brunt of her pain and confusion. But the uncertainty she was feeling had not been lessened by the renewal of their relationship.

CHAPTER SEVEN

JOANNA did not sleep well. Alone in the solitude of her bedroom, she faced the fact that she was the bone of contention here, the stumbling block to Shannon's reunion with his father. So long as she was in the house, there would be no peace for any of them, least of all herself.

The futility of her own feelings left her cold with despair, and she could hardly believe it was only a little over two weeks since she left England, secure in her love for Philip, and his for her. In such a brief space of time, her life had changed completely, and she wished desperately that her father had never sent her on that ill-fated trip to find Shannon.

Shannon! She wiped a tear from the corner of her eye. Just thinking about him brought a physical pain to her chest, and there was no relief to be found in contemplating her proposed marriage. How could she marry Philip, feeling as she knew she did about Shannon? But again, how could she not? No doubt it was the sanest thing to do.

Rolling on to her stomach, she relived again those moments in the airport at Nairobi, remembering Shannon's subsequent denunciation of his parentage. If only it were that simple! If only one could escape one's heredity. If only there was some way ...

But there was not, and no amount of wishing would make it so. And for her father's sake, she must dismiss all thoughts of that kind from her mind. If she could convince Shannon that what had happened between them would never happen again, perhaps he might reconsider. If she went through with her marriage to Philip—and after all, she still loved Philip—surely then Shannon might find it in his heart to stop denying his birthright?

It had been a strange, unnatural evening. Her father had sent for her just after Philip's departure, and when she entered the handsome booklined room where her father spent most of his time, helpless in his wheelchair, she was immediately aware of the antagonism between the two men. That she was the cause of that antagonism made it all that much harder to bear.

As she bent to kiss her father's cold cheek, she was struck again by the dramatic physical change in his appearance. Maxwell Carne had always been a big man, strong and well built, his thick auburn hair flecked here and there with streaks of grey. Now he had shrunk to a mere shadow of his former self, his sudden loss of weight leaving folds of empty skin about his wasted body. He was paralysed completely down one side of his body, but it was a measure of the man's courage that he had not given in to his disability, and had persevered until his speech was almost completely restored. But his hair was now quite white, and the greyish pallor of his skin was all the more pathetic to someone who had shared his love of the outdoors. Yet still his eyes were sharp and alert, and she had the distinct feeling that his brain had overcome its physical shortcomings.

'Hello, Daddy,' she murmured, straightening, flicking an instinctive glance in Shannon's direction. 'How are you?'

'How do you think I am?' muttered Maxwell Carne ungraciously. 'Do vegetables have feelings?'

'You're not a vegetable, Daddy!' Joanna cast another revealing look at Shannon, lounging carelessly against the square oak table which occupied a central position in the room. 'Stop feeling sorry for yourself.'

'Why should I?' Maxwell's voice was bitter. 'No one else cares about me.'

'That's not true!' Joanna spread her hands. 'Why—why, Shannon's made the trip to England, just to see you.'

'Has he?' Maxwell's eyes shifted to his son. 'And why?

Did you know he doesn't intend to stay?'

Although her father's voice was low, Joanna could feel the suppressed emotion behind it, could see the light of defeat in her father's eyes. But defeat would not come easily to him, and she guessed he would fight it all the way. Why couldn't Shannon have waited? she asked herself fiercely. Why couldn't he have allowed her father just a few days ...?

Squaring her shoulders, she said: 'It's early days yet, Daddy. Shannon hasn't really had time——'

'Joanna!' Now Shannon spoke, his face drawn with anger. 'Don't dare to lie about it! There was no point in pretending. *He* knew. I didn't have to lie to him.'

'Why?' Joanna could feel her eyes growing hot with unshed tears. 'Why? I won't believe you have to go back to that place. This is your home!'

'My home!' Shannon's voice was taut with contempt. 'I have no *home*, Joanna. I haven't had for more than ten years!'

'You're a fool!' muttered Maxwell harshly. 'I'm giving you everything—every damn thing!'

'You don't have to buy my silence!' retorted Shannon, with cold emphasis, and Joanna turned to stare at him in dismay. His silence? What silence? What hold did Shannon have over their father?

'For God's sake, man, don't you owe me anything?' Maxwell demanded angrily.

'I don't think so.'

'Daddy!' Joanna could see the threatening colour sweeping up her father's face, and was concerned by it. 'You know what the doctor said——'

'Damn doctors! I'm talking to Shannon. Well? What have you to say for yourself?'

Shannon straightened away from the table, tall and remote. 'I think you should listen to what Joanna says,' he replied steadily.

93

'Damn you!' Maxwell's unparalysed hand gripped convulsively on the arm of his chair, and Joanna turned desperate eyes in Shannon's direction. As though responding to her unspoken appeal, he said frustratedly:

'You must have known you were wasting your time! Why for God's sake couldn't you have employed a manager to run the estate once you knew you'd never run it again?'

'And when I was dead? What then?' Maxwell asked, his voice rising.

Shannon glanced at Joanna. 'You have a daughter. She will have a husband by that time.'

'Do you think I want Philip Lawson to run Mallowsdale?' Maxwell spoke furiously. 'There have always been Carnes at Mallowsdale. You're a Carne, Shannon, whether you like it or not. I want you here!'

Shannon's hands were balled into fists. 'No.'

The fire died out of Maxwell's eyes, and the hectic colour drained away, leaving his face as grey and pallid as ever. Joanna couldn't decide which was worse for him—the excitement, or its aftermath.

'Daddy, we can talk later,' she said, bending to tuck the rug about his legs, but he slapped her hand away.

'Leave it!' he muttered violently. 'Leave it!'

Joanna stood uncertainly, and Shannon moved forward. 'So much concern,' he said scornfully, and she hated him in that moment for his lack of it. 'How curious! Ten years ago my passing scarcely caused a ripple. I wonder why I've become so important.'

Maxwell looked up at him bitterly. 'Ten years ago, I hadn't given up all hope of having a son!'

He almost spat the words, and Joanna was horrified. 'Daddy!'

Shannon had not moved a muscle. 'Let him go on,' he told her grimly. 'Now we're getting nearer the truth.'

Maxwell's hand suddenly hung limp, and Joanna guessed he had almost exhausted his strength. 'You're a hard man,

Shannon,' he said, and she guessed what it cost him to say that.

But strangely, his defeat moved Shannon more surely than his victory would have done. His lips twisting a little at his own vulnerability, Shannon took a deep breath, and then said: 'You told me Lawson's been running things. Exactly what has he done?'

'Why?' Maxwell's heavy brows ascended.

Shannon shook his head. 'Because I find it harder to be like you than I imagined. Make no mistake'—this as his father's lips parted in anticipation, —'I have no intention of staying here. But I am prepared to put the estate in order for some manager to take over, to advise someone else from a purely objective standpoint.'

There was another light in Maxwell's eyes now, and seeing it, Joanna knew that he thought he had won. And he had. This particular battle at least. But the war was by no means over.

The rest of the evening had passed without incident. Philip came back before Shannon came down from his room where he had been unpacking his belongings, and because the two men obviously cared little for one another's company, Joanna suggested that they used the morning room while Shannon talked to her mother in the sitting room. Because of his disability, her father had his bedroom on the ground floor, using what used to be a small dining room. He had a nurse, too, a man in his fifties called Henry Barnes, who was always around when he needed him. On Henry's days off, she and her mother had had to manage, and she knew her father hated that. All the same, he had never allowed Philip to help him, and she wondered whether Shannon would be permitted, or would even want, to do so.

Because of her disturbed night, Joanna slept later than usual, and it was after nine when she opened her eyes and focussed on the clock set on the unit beside her bed. The

95

room was filled with an unnaturally bright light, and she slid out of bed and padded to the window, drawing back the curtains on a world made white and dazzling by snow. The radiator beneath the window was already pumping heat into the room, and she rested her knees against it for a moment, feeling the warmth spreading up her legs to her hips through the thin material of her nightgown.

Her windows overlooked the back of the house where the clutch of outbuildings spread in organised disorder. There were stables and barns, sheds and outhouses for storing tools and machinery, and the building which housed the stainless-steel cooling tank. That was a new innovation, something which Shannon could not have seen. She sighed. Right now it was not in use. Philip had taken the Mallowsdale herd over to High Stoop. It had made things easier for him, and until Shannon—or someone else—took over the running of the estate, they would remain there.

Looking beyond the immediate surroundings of the house, she could see the river, just visible through the trees. Snow had thickened its banks, narrowing the water-course, and she guessed there would be ice clinging to the banks, covered with snow, making it dangerous for anyone to walk there. It was not snowing at the moment, but the sky was grey and overhung, and she thought there would be more later. How strange Shannon must find this landscape after the heat and colour of Africa. She found it different herself, and she had not been long away.

She had showered and was dressing in jeans and a sweater when there was a light tap at her door heralding her mother's entry into the room, carrying a tray of morning tea. In a tweed skirt and knitted jumper, a gingham apron protecting her clothes, Catherine Carne still managed to look vague and rather helpless, and Joanna felt a deepening sympathy for her. She had relied on her father so much, and now he was helpless, too. It had been a terrible shock, much worse for her than for someone more capable of coping for themselves.

'Oh, you're up, Joanna,' she said, with some relief, setting down the tray on the dressing table. 'I hoped you would be. Shannon said to let you lie, but I have to talk to someone or I'll go mad!'

Joanna busied herself with the tea, noticing there were two cups and pouring some for her mother. Catherine took the cup, seated herself on the side of the bed, and looked despairingly at her daughter.

'What is going to become of us?' she exclaimed.

Joanna heaved a sigh. 'Don't be silly, Mummy. What do you mean? What do you think is going to become of us?'

'I don't know. I don't honestly know.' Catherine sipped her tea and shook her head. 'He's not staying, you know. Shannon says he's not staying.'

Joanna turned away and looked out of the window. 'I know.'

'So what are we going to do? Your father can't manage alone. Everything will have to be sold—the herd, the land, this house, everything!'

'Oh, stop it, Mummy! Of course everything won't have to be sold. Nothing's settled yet. Besides, Shannon's promised to stay until everything is sorted out.'

'How can it be sorted out? If he won't stay, what's the point? There's no one else but you, and your father won't let the estate go to the Lawsons. Oh, if only your father had listened to me. He should never have let Shannon go away. But what did he do? Practically forced the boy out of the house. And why? Because of his stupid, overbearing pride!'

Joanna's hands were trembling as she replaced her cup on the tray. 'I expect he—thought it was for the best,' she ventured, wondering how much her mother knew about Shannon's reasons for leaving.

Her mother looked up at her bitterly. 'That's what I've just said. Your father always thought he knew how to handle people. Well, he hasn't made much of a success at

97

it, has he?'

'Oh, Mummy!'

Catherine finished her tea and rose to her feet. 'I've always been a disappointment to your father, I've known that. Producing a girl, instead of the boy he wanted. Never having another child. I should have suspected there might be some excuse for Jacqueline's behaviour. Your father was never the easiest man to live with—to live up to. Poor Shannon! He's certainly been made to pay for his mother's indiscretions.'

Joanna had never heard her mother mention Shannon's mother's name in quite that way before, and she had to bite her tongue to prevent herself from probing further. But now was not the time. She would be taking advantage of a distraught woman, worse—her own mother.

'Well, I'll leave you to finish dressing,' said Catherine, walking wearily towards the door. 'Will you be wanting any breakfast?'

'Perhaps—some toast. But don't you bother, I can get it.' Joanna sighed. 'Where—where's Shannon?'

'I'm not sure. He went out about an hour ago. I believe he's gone to see Charlie Simmons. I suppose he wants to assess the situation for himself before he reports back to your father.'

Joanna absorbed this. 'Yes, I suppose so.'

Catherine halted in the open doorway. 'Oh, Joanna, can't you do something?' she appealed suddenly. 'Shannon always cared about you. Couldn't you influence him? Couldn't you persuade him that he'll kill your father if he goes back to Africa?'

Joanna was aghast. 'I—if Daddy can't convince him——'

'Your father goes at it like a bull at a gate. He has no patience, no time to use tact—and diplomacy. Joanna, you'll be married soon and away from here. How am I going to manage if Shannon abandons us?'

Joanna bent her head, her breathing quickening as panic

enveloped her. 'Mummy, you can't believe that Shannon would listen to me!'

'Why not? You got him to come back here, didn't you? I never thought you'd succeed. But your father appears to know Shannon better than I do.'

'He should do,' protested Joanna tremulously. 'He is his father, after all!'

Catherine's expression hardened slightly. 'Shannon is Jacqueline's son, Joanna, and your father didn't know her very well, did he?'

Joanna shook her head. 'I don't know.'

'No, of course not. You were too young. But take my word for it. Why else——' She broke off suddenly, and when she spoke again, she was calmer. 'You must try, Joanna.'

'Do you think I haven't?' Joanna spread her hands. 'Honestly, it's no use. He doesn't listen to me.'

Catherine turned away. 'I see. Then we must all pray that something happens to change his mind, mustn't we?' she said tightly, and left her.

When she was alone, Joanna sank down weakly on to the side of her bed. Her mother didn't know what she was asking, she thought bitterly, or she would never have suggested such a thing. Obviously she knew nothing of the real reasons for Shannon leaving Mallowsdale. She felt helpless. What could she do? Things had never seemed more desperate.

By the time she went downstairs she had herself in control again, and was even able to exchange a friendly word with Jessie, vacuuming in the sitting room.

'Your father's been asking for you, Joanna,' the daily said, switching off the cleaner as she spoke. 'I told him you weren't up yet, and he said to tell you to come in when you did come down.'

Unaccountably, Joanna's heart sank, and a wave of self-recrimination swept over her. Until her departure for

Africa she had shared a good relationship with her father, and although he shouted at her as he did at everyone, she knew he had a real and deep affection for her. Now, with her prohibitive knowledge, she felt a craven desire to avoid any confrontation alone with him.

But with Jessie smiling at her, obviously waiting for her to go into the library and see her father, she had no choice but to nod and say: 'Thanks, Jessie,' before crossing the hall and tapping at her father's door.

Henry Barnes let her in. He was obviously on his way out, Bess, her father's collie, on a lead in his hand. Joanna had not seen the dog the night before, but now she welcomed the momentary respite, smiling at Henry before bending to fondle the animal.

'Is that you, Joanna?'

Her father's petulant summons tightened the nerves throughout her body, and she exchanged an understanding grimace with Henry before straightening and pushing the door wider.

'Yes, it's me, Father,' she answered, with forced lightness. 'How are you this morning?'

Her father's lips tightened. 'Come in, come in, and close that door,' he ordered, and taking a deep breath, Joanna did as he asked.

'It's been snowing,' she said, unnecessarily, and her father snorted impatiently.

'I had noticed. I'm not blind, you know. Well? I've been waiting to speak to you alone. What happened?'

'What—happened?' Joanna didn't quite understand.

'Between you and Shannon. How did you get him to come back here? What did you tell him? More to the point, what did he say?'

Joanna swallowed hard. Oh, God, she thought sickly, what did he mean? Did he suspect that Shannon...? She licked her dry lips, and endeavoured to behave naturally.

'I—I don't know what you mean. He's here, isn't he?

100

What could he say to me?'

Maxwell had been studying her closely as she spoke, and after a few moments' unnerving examination he seemed to be satisfied that nothing untoward had happened, because he left that subject and attacked another.

'I want those beasts down from High Stoop,' he stated with determination. 'You can tell Lawson I'm grateful for what he's done, but now that Shannon's home——'

'Father, don't you think you ought to wait and hear what Shannon has to say?' she exclaimed in dismay. 'I mean, there's not much point——'

'There's not much point in paying for equipment that's going to waste!' retorted her father shortly. 'We have all the facilities here, we're far more mechanised than Lawson. I want the herd back today, tomorrow at the latest.'

'Daddy, you can't make decisions like that!'

'Why not?'

'Well, because—because Shannon may not be prepared to take charge.'

'Rubbish! Dowsett could have managed on his own if your mother hadn't panicked and gone running to the Lawsons for assistance. Useless creature!'

'Daddy, Dowsett couldn't manage everything. You know that's not true. He's an old man, like—like——'

'Like me!' her father finished for her, and she coloured uncomfortably. 'I know, I know. The Lawsons have the right idea, handing the farm over to Philip. But who have I to hand Mallowsdale on to? You answer me that. Unless Shannon stays.'

Joanna moved restlessly to the windows, looking out on the sweep of drive at the front of the house. Wheel-tracks had churned up the snow here, and the interlacing of footprints of man and beast indicated that Henry Barnes had taken Bess out this way. The tall poplars and elms which lined the drive were bare now, their branches softened by the weight of snow that had lodged upon them, and even

101

the barren hedges displayed a tracery in white.

'Where is he?' Her father was speaking again, and Joanna swung round reluctantly.

'Shannon? He's gone over to the farm to see Charlie Simmons.'

'Huh.' Maxwell sounded irritated. 'Did he say when he'd be back?'

'I don't know. I haven't seen him this morning. Mummy told me. I'm afraid I overslept.'

Maxwell made the jerky movement of his head which signified assent. 'So how was the trip?' he asked, but she had the feeling he was not really interested.

Sighing, she shrugged her slim shoulders. 'It was fine. An education. I enjoyed it.'

Maxwell grimaced. 'It was fine—an education—I enjoyed it!' he mimicked cruelly. 'Is that any way to describe Africa, I ask you?'

Joanna bent her head, pushing her hands deep into the pockets of her jeans. 'It was very hot most of the time, but the hotels were very good. The climate in Johannesburg is quite pleasant, but it was much hotter in Lushasa.'

Her father uttered an oath. 'I don't want to hear about the weather, girl. I can read the forecast any time. I want to hear your impressions of Africa! The dark continent!'

Joanna pursed her lips. 'All right, all right. I didn't like it,' she burst out hotly. 'Not Kwyana, anyway. It's a wild and savage place. Oh, Menawi's all right, I suppose. There are shops and hotels there, but once you leave the city behind you're out in the bush! The roads are terrible. There's no sign of sanitation or civilisation, and people have to struggle just to stay alive! The heat is enervating. It saps your strength. And the insects ...' She shivered, and Maxwell looked well pleased with the results of his probing.

'So you don't consider Africa has more to offer?' he suggested dryly.

'Not for me,' she agreed moodily, half regretting her outburst as her father nodded again. No doubt this was yet another argument which would be used against Shannon.

'So—what are you planning to do today?' he asked, and she tried to gather her thoughts.

'I—I haven't made any plans.'

'But you will be seeing young Lawson?'

'I expect so. His mother wants me to go over there. She's found a pattern for my—my wedding dress.'

Her father was listening, but, she sensed, absently. His unparalysed fingers tapped a tattoo against the wooden arm of his wheelchair, and she guessed he was impatient for Shannon to return. It was strange how determined he was that Shannon should have the estate. Did he regret sending his son away, whatever the reason? Would things fall into perspective once she was married and gone from here? Would Shannon stay that long? She doubted it.

She heard the sound of the Range Rover long before her father did, and when it swept up the drive to the house, she said: 'I think Shannon's back. I expect he'll be coming to see you. I'll go and get some breakfast.'

Maxwell signified his agreement, and she walked quickly across to the door. She had hoped to get away before Shannon appeared, but that proved to be impossible. As she came out of the library, he was coming in the outer door, kicking snow from his boots, unzipping the heavy, fur-lined navy parka he was wearing. She recognised the coat as one belonging to her father, and felt the poignancy of the situation in knowing he would never wear it again. Shannon looked up as she stood hesitantly just outside the library door, and they exchanged a long, unsmiling look. Then he hooked the parka on his thumb, and slinging it over his shoulder, walked towards her.

Joanna stiffened, but remained where she was, even though her strongest instincts were to run. She must not weaken, she told herself fiercely. She must not allow him to see how easily he could disturb her. They were in England

103

now. Those moments in Africa should never have been. For her father's sake, she had to make him see that his place was here, that she was unimportant in the scheme of things.

'Daddy's waiting to see you,' she said, and even to her ears, her voice sounded high and unnatural. 'Is it as cold out as it looks? I didn't feel like getting out of bed this morning. After two weeks in the sun, you really feel the cold, don't you? I suppose it's even worse for you.'

'You look pale,' he said, ignoring her chatter, and she felt that awful feeling of futility in everything she did. 'Did you sleep well?'

'Yes, of course, I slept well,' she replied vehemently, pursuing her course. 'I always sleep well in my own bed. I think everybody does, don't you? I mean, it's what you're used to, isn't it? Did you? Sleep well, I mean?'

Shannon's lips twisted. 'By your criterion, I wouldn't, would I?' he remarked mockingly, and with a brief nod he opened the library door and went inside, closing it firmly behind him.

CHAPTER EIGHT

PHILIP arrived after lunch. Shannon had taken his meal in the library, with Maxwell, and Joanna and her mother were still seated at the kitchen table, lingering over their coffee, when he knocked at the back door.

Joanna sprang up and opened the door to him, reaching automatically to return his kiss. But it was obvious that Philip was not in a good humour, and his embrace was purely perfunctory. As soon as he was able, he transferred his attention to her mother, advancing to the table and demanding bluntly:

'What's all this about Shannon wanting the herd back here? At once?'

Catherine exchanged a look of bewilderment with her daughter. 'The herd, Philip?' she echoed in confusion. 'I—we don't know anything about it. Do we, Joanna?'

Joanna closed the back door and leaned back against it. 'Well, my father did say something about it this morning,' she admitted awkwardly.

Philip snorted. 'Did he? Do I take it that Shannon intends to stay after all?'

'No.' Joanna sighed. 'I don't know what's going on, Philip. You'd better speak to Daddy.'

'I intend to.' Philip shed his sheepskin jacket, and raked a hand through his unruly fair hair. 'We've done what we could for you, Dad and I. We've been neighbours for a few years now, and if neighbours can't help one another in times of trouble, well ... Anyway, if a virtual stranger thinks he can mess us around like this, he's mistaken.'

'I'm sure it wasn't Shannon's intention to mess you around, Philip,' exclaimed Catherine placatingly, getting to her feet. 'Sit down, and have some coffee. It's still hot.'

'I can't stay long, thanks, Mrs Carne.' Philip was looking at Joanna as he spoke, and she guessed he was waiting for her to make some comment in his defence. 'I've got to go out with old Tom. He reckons we've lost seven ewes.'

'Oh, dear.' Catherine shook her head. 'And the snow looks so pretty, too.'

Philip's mouth turned down at the corners. 'Yes—well, if I could just have a few words with your husband, Mrs Carne . . .'

Catherine nodded. 'I'll go and tell him you're here. Joanna, give Philip a cup of coffee. He can drink it while he's waiting.'

The door closed behind her mother, and Joanna moved obediently towards the coffee pot, but Philip stayed her, his fingers closing round her upper arm.

'Never mind about coffee!' he said impatiently. 'Are you coming back with me?'

Joanna shrugged her shoulders. 'I should help Mummy,' she ventured uncomfortably, avoiding his eyes. Even to herself she could not admit that the idea of discussing her wedding dress with his mother filled her with a sense of panic.

'Your mother can manage,' insisted Philip stolidly. 'Come on, I want to talk to you myself.'

Joanna looked up at him then. 'I thought you said your mother wanted to see me, to discuss sewing patterns?'

'And that's what bothered you?' Philip was too astute. But he didn't press her. Instead he went on: 'That was yesterday. Right now, she's too busy caring for the lambs to bother with sewing patterns. No, I thought you might come out with Tom and me. If you get wrapped up. It's cold, but it's bracing. And like your mother says, it is—pretty.'

Joanna hesitated only a moment. It would be nice to get away from the house for a while. She was too close to every-

106

thing here. She couldn't get things in perspective.

'All right,' she said, a smile lifting her lips. 'I'd like to.'

'Good.' Philip let her go. 'Get some boots on, and a thicker sweater. You'll need it.'

Joanna heard Philip's voice as she was coming downstairs again. She could hardly have done otherwise in the circumstances. He was standing in the hall below, practically shouting at Shannon, who was standing facing him, feet slightly apart, his arms folded imperturbably across his chest. From time to time Shannon made some quiet comment, but mostly it was Philip's angry protestations she could hear.

'I'm telling you this, Carne, if you bring the herd back here, I shall wash my hands of the whole damn business!' he was asserting loudly. 'We have enough to do at High Stoop without playing silly beggars with someone who doesn't know when he's well off!'

'That's your prerogative, of course,' Shannon replied mildly. 'As I've told you, Mr Carne makes the decisions around here, not me.'

'I don't believe that. I'm not a fool, you know.' Philip was angry. 'He was happy enough with the arrangements until you came back.'

'He had no choice,' Shannon pointed out steadily. 'Now he has.'

'And when you walk out again—what then?' Philip's lips curled scornfully.

'We'll have to face that hurdle when we come to it,' rejoined Shannon, and then, catching sight of Joanna hesitating uneasily on the stairs, he added: 'Here's your fiancée. Perhaps she'll be able to persuade you that her father has a mind of his own.'

Joanna came reluctantly down the remainder of the stairs, conscious of Shannon's mocking eyes upon her. 'I— I'm ready, Philip,' she said, feeling like an intruder. 'Are you?'

Philip hunched his stocky shoulders. 'I suppose so,' he muttered, but he flashed a venomous glance in Shannon's direction. 'Don't think I'll change my mind either.'

Shannon's arms fell to his sides, and he lifted his shoulders in an indifferent gesture. 'If you'll excuse me, I have work to do,' he said, and turning, walked across the hall to her father's study. He opened the door and let himself inside, and the door closed firmly behind him.

'Look at that!' declared Philip furiously. 'He treats this place just like his—his——'

'—home?' suggested Joanna tautly. 'Well, it is, isn't it?'

'That's not what I meant. That's your father's study, Joanna. Don't you care that he's using it as his own? *He* interviewed me in there. He did! Not your father. Your mother said your father was resting and couldn't be disturbed. I haven't disturbed him other afternoons I've called, have I?'

'Oh, Philip!' Joanna couldn't bear any more of this bickering. 'Come on, let's go out. The afternoons are so short, and I need some air.'

'So do I,' muttered Philip resentfully. 'The air around here stinks!'

It was a childish retaliation, but Joanna forgave him as she followed him to the kitchen to collect his coat. Her father was foolish, acting so precipitately as soon as Shannon got here. Didn't he realise Shannon could walk out again just as precipitately? Did he really think that by heaping responsibilities on his son's head, he could keep him here indefinitely?

Once out in the fields surrounding High Stoop, Joanna was able to forget her own troubles for a while at least. The wind whistling down from the distant fells made it imperative to keep moving, and her boots were soon caked with snow as she struggled to keep up with Philip's longer strides. His dogs, Hector and Lysander, ran on ahead,

108

churning up flurries of snow as they scrabbled about searching for animals buried beneath. Joanna knew that a sheep could survive being buried for a short space of time, and that often ewes had been brought out virtually unharmed. But today they were not so lucky, and the only animal they did find was already stiff and cold.

Back in the kitchen at High Stoop, Mrs Lawson had a pot of tea ready for them on their return. Already darkness was falling, and with it came the drifting flakes of further snow. But it was cosy in the firelit room, crouched about the blazing fire, drinking tea laced with brandy.

'Did you see Mr Carne?' Philip's mother asked presently, and Joanna could feel the tension in the air.

'No.' Philip set his cup down heavily in its saucer. 'I saw Joanna's brother.'

Mrs Lawson glanced at the girl. 'I see.'

Joanna sighed. 'My father does rest sometimes, after lunch,' she murmured. 'And now that Shannon's here——'

'Now that Shannon's here, the old order changeth,' retorted Philip shortly. Then he, too, sighed. 'Oh, leave it, Mother. It's not Joanna's fault. I'll make the arrangements to have the herd driven back tomorrow.'

Mrs Lawson shook her head. 'He's a strange man, your father, Joanna,' she said. 'Ben and Philip—they've done everything they can to help him, and how does he repay us?'

'I said leave it, Mother.'

'I know, I know. But we're not well off, like the Carnes. Oh, we own this bit of land, we scrape a living, and at least when we leave it to you, Philip, you'll be your own master. But we don't have modern machinery, and central heating, and deep freezers ...'

Joanna felt awful. 'Really, Mrs Lawson, my father does appreciate what you've done, honestly. It's just that—well, now that Shannon's home, he's hoping to persuade him to stay. Maybe he thinks if he can get Shannon to take on the responsibilities for the estate ...' She paused, and looked appealingly at Philip. 'Make allowances, please. He's not a well man.'

'There's nothing wrong with Shannon's health,' retorted Philip shortly.

'No, but like he says, my father gives the orders. He's just carrying them out.'

Mrs Lawson poured herself some more tea. 'Well, all I can say is, it's a pity he ever came back,' she said, heavily. 'He's been no son to his father. Why, Philip here has done more for your father during the past eight years than Shannon has. Walking out like that. Caring nothing for any of you. And now I suppose he thinks he can come back and take over.'

'It's not like that at all!' exclaimed Joanna impatiently. 'Shannon doesn't want the estate.'

'What's he going to do then?' demanded Philip. 'Sell it?'

'No. I've told you, he's just—not interested.'

Philip and his mother exchanged a look which Joanna found impossible to comprehend. Then Philip reached out and patted her knee.

'All right, love, don't get upset. I promise not to come to blows with your big brother.' He chuckled rather maliciously. 'Not that I wouldn't like to. That damned high-and-mighty attitude of his! I could push his face in.' He nodded. 'But I won't.'

Joanna sipped her tea, wondering why the victory seemed so hollow somehow. It was what she wanted, after all— Philip to come to terms with Shannon. But as for Philip pushing Shannon's face in—that was something else. She had the distinct feeling that while Philip might be more solidly built than the other man, those hard muscles she had felt when she was in Shannon's arms might well be able to resist anything that her fiancé might throw at him.

It was almost a relief when Mrs Lawson changed the subject, even though it was to discuss the wedding. She got up and rummaged through a drawer and came out with a

110

rather grubby-looking pattern. Mrs Lawson was not the most meticulous of housekeepers, and Joanna knew she would have quite a task ahead of her when she took over the running of the household in June. High Stoop was not as old a building as Mallowsdale, but it had not received the care and attention of the old Hall, and consequently there were a number of things needing attention, not least, the general cleanliness of the place.

'There. What do you think of that?'

Mrs Lawson dropped the sewing pattern into Joanna's lap and she set down her cup and picked it up. On the front of the folder was a picture of the dress to be made from the pattern inside, and despite some tea or coffee stains smudged across the skirt, Joanna could see that it was an attractive style. The neckline was high and cuffed, and the skirt flared from a gathering under the bustline in a slightly mediaeval style. Long sleeves with pointed cuffs added to this illusion, and the headdress the girl was wearing in the picture resembled a small coronet, edged with pearls.

'I—it's beautiful,' she said honestly. 'Where did you find it?'

'In a little remnant house in Carlisle. It's quite an old pattern, I think. I've looked through the latest catalogues and there's nothing quite like it.'

Joanna nodded, looking down at the picture again. She was tall enough to carry such a style, and she knew that Mrs Lawson had the ability to make it. Perhaps she could even find a headdress something like this one, and if she piled her hair up on top of her head ...

She brought herself up short. This was her wedding dress, she was thinking about, her wedding *day*. The day when she gave up being Joanna Carne and became Mrs Philip Lawson instead. It was a daunting prospect. Was marriage to Philip what she really wanted? And wasn't it a bit late now to start having doubts? If only ...

'I thought perhaps crêpe—or ivory damask,' Mrs Lawson was suggesting thoughtfully. 'And you're going to have our Janice's two as bridesmaids, aren't you?'

Janice was Philip's sister who was already married and lived in Lancaster. She had two little girls, Shelley and Elizabeth, and Mrs Lawson was keen that they should be part of the ceremony.

Joanna could feel the ground slipping away from under her feet. There was something inevitable about the plans for a wedding. Once they were set in motion, they gathered momentum on the way, and every action had a reaction until one had the feeling that one was being propelled onward almost against one's will.

'I think they'll look best in pink or lilac,' Mrs Lawson was saying now, resuming her seat by the fire. 'Neither of them suit deep colours, and in any case, you don't want definite colours at a wedding, do you?'

Philip was waiting expectantly for Joanna to make her own feelings known, and she forced herself to take an active part in the conversation.

'I'd like to discuss it with Mummy first,' she said, seeking a respite. 'She's rather good at choosing colours and things. And I'd like her to see the pattern before making any definite decision.'

'Well, we've got to start thinking about it, Joanna,' said Mrs Lawson rather sharply. 'There are only about fifteen weeks left, you know. And this is our busiest time of the year. If you want me to make the dresses for you, you'll have to come to a decision soon.'

'Oh, I will, I will.' Joanna moved her shoulders apologetically.

'I mean, I have to know,' went on Mrs Lawson, almost as if Joanna hadn't spoken. 'You dashing off to Africa like that didn't help, did it? And with your father being ill and all ... We've all had to help out, and helping out takes time.'

'I know that, Mrs Lawson, and I'm very grateful, honestly——'

'Well, that's more than can be said for some!' commented a harsh voice from the doorway, and Joanna shivered in the cold draught of air emitted by the entry of Philip's father, a new-born lamb clasped in his brawny arms.

Her sympathetic delight in seeing the lamb hid the aversion she always felt in Ben Lawson's presence. She didn't like Philip's father, she never had, a feeling which had intensified on the one occasion he had cornered her in the milking shed and run familiar hands over her thighs. When she had slapped his hands away he had pretended he had been having a joke with her, but Joanna had known better. Now she avoided his company whenever possible.

Ben put the lamb down on the hearth and it promptly struggled to get to its feet. But weakness and exhaustion overcame its efforts, and Mrs Lawson went to heat it up some milk.

'The ewe's dead,' announced Ben, in answer to Philip's questioning stare. 'That makes four today, and it's snowing again.'

Joanna got to her feet. 'I ought to be going, Philip,' she said quickly. 'If it's snowing . . .'

Ben shrugged off his thick anorak and slung it carelessly over the back of a chair. 'What have you got to go dashing off home for? You don't have any ewes lambing, do you?' he challenged her.

Joanna made a helpless gesture. 'No—but if it's snowing——'

'You're not going to get snowed in or anything. Sit down, sit down, lass.' He came to seat himself in the deep armchair his wife had previously been occupying beside Joanna, and began to tug off his boots. 'You can't go running away as soon as I come in.'

'I am not running away, Mr Lawson,' declared Joanna forcefully, her dislike of him stiffening her resolve. 'But I am going home.'

'Oh, ay?' Ben stretched his feet towards the fire. 'Well,

113

you can tell that young devil of a brother of yours a message from me——'

'Father! We've been into all that,' exclaimed Philip, quellingly, but his father was not to be put off.

'You can tell him that when you and Philip are married, I'll stand no truck with his arrogance. We'll be family then, my girl, and he won't make me the laughing stock of Mallowsdale again.'

'I'm sure Shannon had no intention——'

'Didn't he?' Ben sought about his person for his pipe, a disreputable object in which Joanna was sure he burned anything he could lay his hands on. He jammed the pipe between his teeth, and lighting a spill in the fire, he added: 'You just give him the message. Let me be the judge as to what his intentions are.'

Philip drove Joanna back to the Hall in his Land-Rover. It was snowing quite heavily now, and it caked on the wipers, making visibility difficult. But when she suggested she could walk the rest of the way, he wouldn't hear of it, and drove her right up the drive to the front door.

'Are you coming in?' she asked, half hoping he would refuse, and when he did, perversely wishing he had not.

'No,' he said. 'I'd better get back. And—well, don't take too much notice of what Dad says, will you? I mean, it's natural that he should feel bitter.'

Joanna hesitated a moment, and then leant across and pressed a kiss to his lips, welcoming his arms around her for the first time since her return from Africa. This was where she belonged, she told herself determinedly, this was the man she loved, the man she was going to marry. Anything else was pure madness.

'Don't worry,' she said now, snuggling against him. 'This weather is making everyone irritable.'

Philip hugged her close. 'I'd be less irritable if we had more time alone together,' he spoke into her hair, pushing back her hood so that its silky curtain fell about her

114

shoulders. 'It was bad enough before, but since your father's stroke ...' He sighed. 'Never mind, it will soon be June, and then I'll have you to myself for all time.'

The awful inevitability of his words brought a chill down Joanna's spine. Fifteen weeks, that was what his mother had said. Fifteen more weeks—and then a lifetime's commitment. It was too much to consider right at this moment.

Pulling herself away from him, she brushed back her hair. 'I'd better go in,' she said. 'Daddy will have heard the sound of the engine and will be wondering what's going on.'

'Surely he'll know,' retorted Philip dryly. 'Joanna, sooner or later, your father has got to realise that you're not his possession any longer.'

'I know,' Joanna nodded, as she climbed out, raising her hand in farewell as he adjusted the gears and reversed away down the drive. She waited until the lights of the vehicle had disappeared before mounting the steps and entering the house.

The door to her father's study was open, and to her surprise she could hear the sound of voices from within, Shannon's and someone else's, a young, feminine voice, which from time to time dissolved into fits of giggles.

Curiosity made her cross the hall before taking off her parka, and she hesitated outside the study door, listening to the exchange going on inside. She wasn't consciously aware of eavesdropping until Jessie came out of the kitchen, but then her cheeks flamed as the daily woman raised her eyebrows knowingly.

'It's young Tracy,' she told Joanna easily. 'Charlie Simmons' girl. You know she's working for Websters, the estate agents. Well, she's a shorthand typist, and seeing that she's on holiday for a few days, Shannon suggested she might like to come up here and give him a hand sorting out your father's correspondence and so on, and earn a bit of cash into the bargain. Tracy fair jumped at the chance. After all, there's not a lot to do on holiday at this time of the year, is there?'

Joanna could feel her nails digging into the palms of her hands, and she knew the desire to draw blood. But not her own. She would fain have liked to walk into that study and order them both out of there, but her excuse that they were intruding on her father's privacy did not quite ring true, even to her ears.

Instead she said tightly: 'I could have helped him,' and turning away, began to unzip her coat.

'I didn't know you were a shorthand typist, Joanna.'

Shannon had heard their voices and come to investigate himself, and now he stood in the open doorway, lean and disturbingly masculine in close-fitting black corded pants and a fine knitted shirt in dark red wool.

'I'm not.' Joanna faced him defensively. 'I just think you might have—have mentioned your intentions to me.'

'Consulted you, you mean?' he suggested dryly. 'I'm afraid that thought didn't cross my mind. But if you have some objection to Tracy coming here ...'

The girl had appeared behind him. Joanna remembered her well enough. She was the Simmons' eldest daughter. She would be perhaps nineteen or twenty now, fresh from secretarial college, and like most girls of her age, full of confidence. She was not normally as tall as Joanna, but the wedge heels she was wearing added a couple of inches to her height, and a tight-fitting sweater and French slim pants completed her ensemble.

'Hello, Joanna,' she called, her smug expression revealing she had overheard Joanna's interchange with Shannon. 'You don't mind me helping out, do you?'

Put like that, Joanna could not object without being rude. Her eyes sought Shannon's, but the detachment she found there was almost her undoing. Those moments in Nairobi might never have been. And to think she was the one who had been thinking she would have to convince *him* that it would never happen again!

116

'I—no. No, of course I don't mind, Tracy,' she replied shortly. She took off her coat and hooked it over the banister. 'If you'll excuse me, I—I want to change before tea.'

CHAPTER NINE

DURING the following week Joanna saw little of Shannon. When he wasn't out about the estate with Murray Dowsett or Charlie Simmons, he was closeted in the study with Tracy, sorting out her father's correspondence, and putting the accounts in order. It was remarkable what had accumulated during the two months of her father's illness, and he spent so much time indoors that even his tan started to fade.

Joanna could not help but be concerned about him. She knew, better than any of them, that he had only just recovered from a debilitating attack of malaria, and the effect on his system of transferring from a tropical climate to an extremely cold one could not be ignored. There were lines on his face which had not been there before, and she thought he could not be sleeping well. At times he looked quite haggard, but this added to, rather than detracted from his dark attraction.

At the beginning of the following week Tracy had to return to her own job in Carlisle, and coming downstairs one morning a couple of days later, Joanna was amazed at the relief she felt, knowing the girl was no longer in the house.

Mrs Carne was in the kitchen, reading the morning paper. Jessie had not yet arrived, and Joanna plugged in the toaster, going to the larder to cut herself some bread.

'Has it been snowing again?' she asked, frowning, as she waited for the toaster to eject its contents.

Her mother dragged herself away from the article she was reading with obvious reluctance. 'What? Oh, yes, I think so.' Catherine looked towards the windows with resigned eyes. 'I was going into Carlisle today, to do some shopping, but the roads are so bad, and Shannon doesn't have time to take me.'

'Shall I?' suggested Joanna, starting as the bread popped out of the machine behind her. 'I don't mind.'

'No, thank you, dear. You know I don't like being driven by another woman.' Catherine folded her paper. 'No, I shall just stay at home and do some baking instead. The freezer needs re-stocking with pies and pastries.'

Joanna buttered the toast, and spooned marmalade into the centre. 'As you like.'

Catherine put the paper aside and got to her feet. 'Joanna,' she paused, 'Joanna, has Shannon said anything more to you? About leaving, I mean?'

Joanna concentrated on the toast. 'No. But then he hasn't said anything to me at all. I hardly ever see him. Why? Has he spoken to you?'

'No. That's just the point. I'm afraid your father is beginning to depend on him. I think he really believes that when it comes to the crunch, Shannon will stay.'

Joanna chewed determinedly at the toast, but it might as well have been sawdust in her mouth for she hardly tasted it. 'I shouldn't bank on that, Mummy, if I were you,' she mumbled, licking crumbs from her lips. 'There's been a lot to catch up on, that's all. As soon as everything's in order ...'

'You think he'll go?'

Joanna shrugged. 'That's what he said.'

'But he *can't*!' Catherine paced desperately around the kitchen, wringing her hands. 'Oh, Joanna, if he does, what's going to become of us?'

Joanna had lost her appetite. She pushed the toast aside, reaching instead for the coffee pot standing by her mother's plate. Its still warm contents were a mild stimulant. 'Mummy!' she exclaimed. 'We've already been into all this.'

'But don't you see, Joanna? Something has to be done.

Shannon's already been here ten days. How long do you suppose he's prepared to remain?'

'I don't know, Mummy. Why don't you ask him?'

Catherine sighed. 'I've asked your father, and he won't even listen to me. He just tells me to mind my own business.'

Joanna lay back wearily in her chair. 'Ask Shannon, then.'

Catherine shook her head, staring unseeingly through the kitchen window. 'I can't. I'm afraid—I'm afraid that if I do, I'll precipitate some action on his part, and if your father ever found out . . .'

Joanna pushed back her chair and stood up. 'Well, we'll all just have to wait, then, won't we?'

Catherine turned. 'You could ask him, Joanna? Just—just casually, you know. He might take it from you.'

'Oh, Mummy!' Joanna could not reassure her. 'Just leave it, hmm? We'll know soon enough.'

Jessie's arrival gave her the opportunity to escape, and she stood in the hall for a few moments, breathing deeply, not quite knowing what she was going to do. Then, on impulse, she crossed to the study door and tapped lightly on the panels.

There was no sound from within, so she opened the door. She had not expected Shannon to be there. At this hour of the morning he would still be down at the milking sheds, and closing the door behind her, she approached her father's desk.

The untidy mixture of letters and bills had gone. Most of the letters had been answered and filed, but those that still required attention reposed in the metal trays provided. The account books were stacked in a neat pile, and even the blotter contained a fresh sheet of paper.

Sighing, she walked round the desk and seated herself in her father's shabby leather chair. When she was younger, she had been allowed to come in here to do her homework, and she had enjoyed the feeling of importance it had given her. But now she just felt a sense of poignancy that her father would never be able to sit here again. And his only son was rejecting the position.

She pulled open one of the drawers beside her. There was her father's fountain pen—he abhorred ballpoints—several pencils, sharpened to a fine point, a box of paper clips and a stapling machine. Simple, impersonal things, and yet they signified so much. There was a dictionary, too. Spelling was not one of her father's strong points, and he always liked to check on any word he was doubtful about. She flicked it open, idly thumbing through the pages, and almost involuntarily found herself looking for one particular word. Yes, there it was—*Sibling*: two or more children, with one or both parents in common . . .

The opening of the door startled her, and she was annoyed at the guilty flush which spread up her cheeks at Shannon's entrance. Annoyed, too, at the angry expression he assumed when he saw her there.

'What are you doing?' he demanded harshly, and indignation imprisoned her in her seat when her instincts had been to leave.

'I don't think I have to explain my actions to you,' she retorted, dropping the dictionary back into the drawer and closing it, suppressing the impulse to slam it, hard.

Shannon closed the door and leaned back against it. 'Have you been checking up on me?'

Joanna's flush deepened. 'No. No, of course not. Besides . . .' She had to be honest. 'I wouldn't know how.'

'Your father should have ensured you had a working knowledge of the estate,' he said, straightening. 'You obviously have little else to do.'

Joanna's eyes widened. 'Are you criticising me?'

Shannon shrugged, hooking his thumbs into the low belt of his black jeans. 'Most girls have an occupation of some sort. What do you do?'

121

'Nothing. As you've pointed out.' Joanna hunched her shoulders.

'Why not? As I recall, you were doing reasonably well with your school work when I left home.'

'Thanks very much.' Joanna was sarcastic.

'Well?'

'I left school when I was eighteen with seven "O" levels and two "A" levels,' she stated defiantly, holding up her head. 'I wanted to be a journalist, but Daddy wouldn't allow it. So I got a job as a shop assistant in Carlisle.'

'A shop assistant?'

'Yes.' Joanna pursed her lips. 'It may have escaped your notice, but jobs aren't too thick on the ground around here. Anyway, as I say, I got a job as a shop assistant, but—well, I got fired.'

'Why?'

Joanna shrugged. 'This and that.'

'People can't get fired that easily.'

'Oh, all right. The manager became too friendly, and his wife arranged for me to be replaced. Does that satisfy you?'

Shannon's expression had hardened. 'And after?'

'Daddy said he needed me around here, to answer the telephone and take messages and so on. You know what he's like. He didn't like me working. Perhaps he was afraid I might do what you'd done.'

Shannon advanced towards the desk. 'But he didn't teach you agricultural practice.'

'No. He saved that for you.' Joanna lifted her shoulders in a dismissing gesture. 'Oh, I've got no excuse. I was over age. I could have done what I wanted, but——'

'Your father bullied you as he tries to bully everyone else,' stated Shannon flatly, resting his palms on the desk in front of her. 'I know. It's easier to give in.'

'Maybe I'm just basically lazy,' said Joanna, supremely aware of the fact that if she leant forward her face would be only inches from his.

'You don't really believe that,' retorted Shannon, long lashes veiling the expression in his eyes. 'So what are you really doing in here?'

Joanna bent her head. 'I thought that—that now—that girl's gone, you might need some assistance.'

'You mean Tracy, of course.'

'Who else?'

'Exactly. So why not come out and say so, instead of *that girl*? She was very useful to me.'

'I'll bet she was.'

'Joanna!' His voice had roughened, and a shiver of anticipation ran down her spine. 'Don't be a fool!' He straightened away from the desk, walking towards the window, his hands thrust deep into the pockets of his pants. After a few moments he went on: 'Most of what had to be done is done. But I'm going to arrange for Percy Lacey, your father's accountant, to come and take a look at things.'

Joanna looked at the broad back he had turned to her, the way his hair grew low on his neck, overlapping the collar of his black denim shirt, the width of his shoulders, the tapering towards his waist, the lean, muscular hips. The desire to touch him was suddenly almost a physical pain, but she remained where she was, fighting the insanity she was contemplating. Then he turned, and she saw how much paler he had become, but she kept her head down so that he should not see what was in her eyes.

'So?' he said expressionlessly. 'What are you planning to do today?'

'I don't know.' Joanna glanced up at him. 'You look tired, Shannon. You should rest more. You're driving yourself too much. You forget—you've been ill.'

'I don't—forget anything,' he retorted briefly. Then: 'I want to go over to Penrith this morning. Do you want to come?'

Joanna's hands clung together. 'I—aren't the road very bad for travelling?'

'You don't have to come,' he replied steadily. 'It's up to you.'

Joanna's heart was beating that much faster, and her breathing had quickened automatically. 'Do—do you want me to come?'

A look of resignation crossed his face. 'Stop it, Joanna,' he advised with some asperity. 'I merely thought you might enjoy the opportunity to do some shopping. You haven't been out much since you got home.'

Joanna rested her elbow on the desk, supporting her head with her upturned hand. 'I—Mummy said you didn't have time to take her into Carlisle.'

'I don't. But I want to go to the bank in Penrith. Your mother wants to go shopping. I told her she was welcome to come along, but she refused. Obviously the shops in Penrith are not good enough for her.'

Treacherously, Joanna was glad. She didn't want to have to share these precious minutes of his time with anyone.

'Well, I—I'd like to come,' she murmured, tracing a pattern on the blotter with her finger nail. She looked up. 'When are we leaving?'

'As soon as you're ready,' he replied, folding his arms. 'I shouldn't bother changing. The town is bound to be thick with slush, and it's filthy walking.'

Joanna straightened and got to her feet. 'All right.' Her eyes sought his. 'You—I mean—you're not regretting asking me, are you?'

Shannon brushed past her as she walked towards the door, swinging it open for her. 'It'll be no Sunday school treat, Joanna. Just something to pass a couple of hours for you.'

Joanna was offended by his tone. 'I don't need indulging!' she asserted hotly, and felt angry when his mouth twisted sardonically.

'Don't you? Then why do you indulge yourself?'

124

She gasped, 'I don't!'

'I think you do,' he retorted. 'Oh, get your coat, Joanna, and stop playing silly games. You'd better tell your mother where you're going, and she can tell your father.'

'You could do that,' she exclaimed, nodding towards the library door. 'While I get my coat.'

'Just tell your mother,' advised Shannon briefly, and although she would have stood and argued, common sense warned her that if she did so, he would simply go without her. And whatever happened, she could not risk that. So, taking a deep breath, she marched away towards the kitchen, aware that he went back into the study and closed the door.

It was only a little over twelve miles to Penrith, but although the snow ploughs had been out since early morning, in places the road was reduced to a single lane. Consequently, their progress was delayed, and it was after eleven when they came down through Skelton into the narrow one-way streets of the small market town. Despite the weather, it being market day, Penrith was crowded, but pedestrians clung to the footpaths, avoiding the spray of melting snow thrown up by passing vehicles. Shannon had to slow the Range Rover to a crawl as they drove up and down Brunswick Road and Middlegate looking for somewhere to park, eventually squeezing into the space left by a departing station wagon near the railway station. Then he turned to his passenger.

'What are you going to do, Joanna? I want to go to the bank first, but we could meet for coffee afterwards, if you like.'

Joanna hid her disappointment. 'I—well, will you be long in the bank?'

'I hope not.'

'Then couldn't I come with you?'

'Don't you want to do any shopping?'

Joanna sighed. 'Not specially.'

Shannon looked as though he was going to say something, and then changed his mind. But she knew what he was thinking. He had been about to ask her why she had come in that case, but had guessed what her answer would be and avoided it.

'I think it would be better if we arranged to meet in—say, half an hour?' he suggested at last, consulting the plain gold watch on his wrist. 'I have to see the bank manager, and you'd only be bored. Go buy yourself a book, or something. Some perfume. Where could we meet for coffee?'

Joanna looked down at her hands, folded in her lap. 'Well, there's a place called Look Inn,' she volunteered reluctantly. 'In King Street.'

'Fine. I think I know where that is. In any case, I'll find it. The old place doesn't change that much, and I do remember most of it.'

Joanna gave him brief directions, and he nodded, then thrust open his door and climbed out. Joanna did likewise, and waited while he locked the vehicle.

'Come on,' he said. 'I'll walk back to the market place with you. Then we'll go our separate ways until what?—a quarter to twelve? Is that suitable to you?'

Joanna shrugged. 'Whatever you say.'

The suppressed oath Shannon uttered under his breath warned Joanna she had said enough. They walked back along Castlegate in silence, and after a brief word of farewell he left her.

For a few moments she felt lost, looking about her through eyes stinging with ridiculous unshed tears. But the coldness got to her eventually, and as she had no desire to stand about listening to the market vendors extolling their wares at the tops of their voices, she skirted the canvas-covered stalls and turned into the nearest store. She didn't expect to see anyone she knew, and she wandered aimlessly through the various departments, merely filling in time until she was due to go and meet Shannon.

She was admiring a swathe of printed silk draped becomingly about a plaster model when a familiar voice caused her heart to sink rather alarmingly to the bottom of her stomach. Just beyond the model was a stand displaying several different types of cloth, and Philip's mother was lingering beside it, discussing the merits of a length of jersey with the sales assistant.

Joanna's immediate instinct was to turn her back and walk quickly away, hoping Mrs Lawson would not notice her, but before she could formulate a decision, one way or the other, the woman had looked up and seen her, eyes stretching delightedly.

'Joanna!' she called, excusing herself from the sales girl, and coming towards her. 'I didn't know you were coming to Penrith today.'

Joanna forced a smile. 'I didn't know myself, actually. But Shannon had to come in, and he asked if I'd like to come along.'

Mrs Lawson's lips thinned. 'Oh, you're with him.' She glanced round. 'Where is he?'

Joanna shook her head. 'He had some business to attend to, so I'm just shopping around on my own.'

'Oh, I see.' The older woman brightened again. 'Well, what an opportunity this is.'

'An opportunity? An opportunity for what?' Joanna didn't understand.

Mrs Lawson spread her hand. 'Here—in this department. All this material. Joanna, come over here. I'm sure this satin damask——'

'Oh, really, Mrs Lawson,' Joanna could feel that awful sense of panic again, 'I really think my mother should be present when I choose the material for my wedding dress.'

Mrs Lawson sighed irritably. 'You've shown her the pattern, haven't you?'

'Well—yes.'

'So what did she say?'

'I think she liked it.' Joanna moved uncomfortably, shifting her weight from one foot to the other. 'But honestly, Mrs Lawson, until something's settled about the estate, I don't think she's got a lot of interest in anything.'

'But it could be months before something's settled about that estate!'

'I don't think so.' Joanna wished she did not have to say the actual words. 'Shannon—Shannon will have to decide soon what he's going to do. He—he has his job in Lushasa to consider.'

Mrs Lawson sounded unconvinced. 'Well, if he's going back there, who's going to run Mallowsdale?'

'We don't know,' said Joanna tightly. 'That's why—that's why my mother is so—so unsettled.'

'Huh.' Mrs Lawson squared her ample shoulders. She was very like Philip to look at, sturdy and uncompromising. 'Well, I think your father's being very silly, making an enemy of Philip. One day he'll have to eat his words, you mark what I say.'

'Oh, Mrs Lawson, Daddy's not making an enemy of anyone, at least, not intentionally.'

'That's not what I think. Anyway, if you're not interested in making plans for the wedding, perhaps you ought to tell Philip.'

Joanna tugged impatiently at a strand of silky hair. 'It's not that I'm not interested, Mrs Lawson . . .'

'Isn't it?' Mrs Lawson shook her head. 'I don't know what it is, Joanna. I can't just put my finger on it. But you've been a different person since that brother of yours came home. It seems to me he's been poisoning your mind against us, and I think that's most unfair.'

'But he hasn't!' exclaimed Joanna desperately. 'But—well, didn't you have any doubts, Mrs Lawson, before you got married?'

'You're having doubts, are you?' Mrs Lawson's back was really up now. 'Well, I don't know. After the way our

Philip's run around after you—made an idol of you, he has, and how do you repay him? By having doubts!'

Joanna looked round, feeling more uncomfortable than ever when she realised the number of speculative glances being cast in their direction.

'I didn't mean—that is, you don't understand, Mrs Lawson.'

'You're right, I don't. And I haven't got the time to stand here arguing with you all day either. I've got a home to run, and a family to feed. Perhaps if you had a bit more to do you'd have less time to think about yourself!'

And with that, she walked away, ample hips swinging with righteous indignation.

Joanna expelled her breath on a low whistle, and colouring as she found sympathetic eyes still upon her, she moved out of sight behind a rack of haberdashery, making a concentrated examination of a packet of safety pins as though her life depended on it.

By the time she had made her way out of the store, it was time to go and meet Shannon, and she walked quickly along the slushy street, her cheeks still burning. He was already there when she reached the coffee bar, waiting outside, hands thrust deep into the pockets of his parka. But at least he seemed to have shed his earlier impatience, and they went inside to squeeze their way through the press of people to the bar.

'You look flushed,' he commented, fishing some change out of his pocket as the waitress pushed beakers of steaming coffee across the counter towards them.

'It's the cold air,' said Joanna, wrapping her hands round the hot glass encased in its metal holder.

'Is it?' Shannon sounded sceptical, but he didn't argue, merely raised his coffee to his lips in a brief salute. 'I can't say I like this place. It's too crowded. Do you fancy drinking this and then calling in somewhere for a bar lunch on our way home?'

'That sounds nice,' Joanna nodded, trying to put all thoughts of Philip's mother out of her mind and not really succeeding. 'Did—er—did you have a successful visit to the bank?'

'If by that you mean did I get what I wanted, then yes, I suppose I did,' replied Shannon quietly. 'What did you do?'

'Oh, nothing much.' Joanna bent her head, glad of the curtain of her hair to hide her face. 'I went into Bell and Palmers, actually. Just window shopping.'

'Did you see anyone you know?'

Shannon was too astute, and Joanna couldn't lie to him. 'As—as a matter of fact, I met Philip's mother,' she said.

'Did you?'

Shannon's eyes narrowed, but she was relieved when he made no further comment. Instead, he concentrated on finishing his coffee, and she did the same.

It was a pleasure to get outside again, even if it was much colder. It was not a long walk back to the Range Rover, but Joanna was relieved when they were safely inside, and Shannon was reversing out of the narrow parking area.

They were accelerating up the long climb out of the town when Shannon disconcerted her by asking: 'So what did Mrs Lawson say to make you look so flustered?'

Joanna bit her lip hard before replying. Then she said honestly: 'I—she—we were discussing the material for my—my wedding dress.'

'I see.' Shannon swung out to pass a slow-moving lorry. 'When are you getting married? Has the date been set?'

'Not—not exactly. It's June, but we haven't actually decided which day.'

Shannon slowed as they negotiated a roundabout, and then added: 'So why should that upset you?'

'It didn't upset me,' she protested.

'Oh, don't give me that. I know you too well, Joanna. Something else was said. Was it to do with me?'

Joanna resented his tone. 'Why should it be to do with

you? You're not the only topic of conversation around here! Mr Lawson's right. You are—*arrogant*!'

'Is that what he said?'

Joanna flushed. 'Not today. I haven't seen Mr Lawson today.'

'From that I can take it that I've been the topic of conversation on other occasions,' remarked Shannon dryly, and she gave him a resentful look.

'You're so clever, aren't you?' She pursed her lips. 'All right, as a matter of fact, your name was mentioned today.'

'Surprise, surprise.'

'Don't be sarcastic!' Joanna bent her head. 'Mrs Lawson thinks I'm wasting too much time. That I should be making more effort towards arranging the wedding. I told her that Mummy was too worried right now to show much interest in that sort of thing, and she asked what we would do when you left.'

'And what did you tell her?'

'What could I tell her? I said I didn't know what we were going to do yet. It's the truth. I don't.'

'You could have told her to mind her own business,' he said, using the windscreen washers as dirt was thrown up from a passing car.

Joanna was horrified. 'I couldn't do that! The Lawsons have been very good to us since Daddy had his stroke. Besides,' she paused, 'she already thinks I've changed since you came home. That would really settle the issue.'

Shannon frowned. 'Perhaps that would be as well.'

'What do you mean?'

'I'm not sure you should marry Philip Lawson.'

'What?'

'You heard me. I mean it.'

Joanna's heart pounded. 'You mean—you mean——' She turned towards him in her seat. '*You*—don't want me to marry Philip?'

Shannon shook his head, his expression discouraging. 'I

131

don't like him,' he said. 'I wouldn't want any—relative of mine to marry him.'

'Oh, Shannon!' Joanna swung round in her seat, her lips working silently. 'You really like to hurt me, don't you?'

'I'm being honest with you,' he stated uncompromisingly. 'I can't say more than that. Besides, your father will never allow Mallowsdale to fall into Lawson's hands. If you were marrying someone else, it might be different.'

'Mallowsdale's yours, Shannon! No one else's.'

'And I don't want it,' retorted Shannon coldly. 'Get that through your head, Joanna. Because I meant it when I left Kwyana, and I still mean it now.'

Tears welled up into Joanna's eyes. 'But—but what will we do?'

Shannon's hands tightened on the wheel, white knuckles showing through his tan. 'I've already advertised for a manager in the Carlisle *Gazette*,' he replied, and all hope seemed to leave her at that moment. 'I should be getting some replies in a few days. As soon as I find someone suitable, someone I can brief in a couple of weeks, I'll be returning to Africa.'

CHAPTER TEN

THEY stopped for lunch at the Green Man in Little Bowsdale. A watery sun was forcing its way through the clouds as if in defiance of Joanna's misery, and the small bar lounge was bright and cosy with its blazing log fire. A fox's head was mounted on the wall, and antlers were stretched above the mantel, horse brasses shining where the rays of sun caught them.

There was a choice of menu—sandwiches, pies, or chicken in a basket. Joanna chose a cheese sandwich, uncaring what she ate, and Shannon carried a pork pie back to their table near a low banquette in the corner. There were not many people in the bar at this hour of the afternoon, and those there were were engrossed in their own affairs.

'This is one thing I miss in Kwyana,' remarked Shannon, indicating the pie. 'Meat is usually served fresh. It's the safest way.'

Joanna chewed a mouthful of her sandwich, helping it down with gulps of the lager he had provided her with. 'You must like Africa very much,' she mumbled, avoiding his eyes.

'I like the people I work with,' he conceded. 'They're a fine bunch of men. Completely fearless, most of them. They have to be.'

'What you mean is—the risks are great,' she told him, her lips trembling.

'No greater than in other forms of mining.'

'I don't believe that. I can remember there being a disaster at a gold mine in South Africa——'

'There are disasters everywhere,' he retorted forcefully. 'It was a disaster when there was an earthquake in Turkey,

133

when that airliner came down in Peru—disasters are not confined to the mining industry.'

'The incidence of them is greater.'

'I disagree. Joanna, if it's decreed that I'll die in a mining accident, then so be it. You can't escape your fate.'

'I didn't know you were a fatalist.'

'I didn't used to be. But experience changes things.'

'So why did you say your men need to be fearless?'

Shannon shook his head. 'You're talking about death, Joanna. I'm talking about life. Some of my men work at depths of up to almost ten thousand feet. A man needs nerves of steel to do that.'

'Or no imagination.'

'If you like.'

Joanna's sandwich had become distasteful to her. 'And does this new belief you have show no compassion for the people who care about you?' she choked.

'We each have our own lives to live, Joanna. Don't try to tell me how to live mine.'

It was freezing when they came out of the pub, their breath vapourising in the sharp air. The Green Man stood on the outskirts of the village, and all around them was that special cloak of silence that snow seems to bring. Expanses of white spread on all sides, and a snow-smudged sign indicating the footpath leading to a circle of stones pointed aimlessly.

However, when Joanna would have gone and climbed into the Range Rover again, Shannon paused, indicating the signpost reminiscently. 'Keld Beacon!' he exclaimed. 'God, it's years since I've thought of that.' He smiled. 'Do you remember when I took you camping there, that summer when your father wouldn't allow you to go to Belgium with the school?'

Joanna pushed her hands into her pockets. 'Yes, I remember,' she nodded, without enthusiasm.

Shannon sighed. 'Let's go up there. Just for old times'

134

sake. We could do it in less than twenty minutes.'

'So you can say farewell?' asked Joanna bitterly.

'If that's the way you want it—yes.'

Joanna shrugged indifferently. 'All right, I've got no objections. But you told Mummy you had no time to waste.'

Shannon regarded her with resignation. 'Stop being awkward, Joanna. If you don't want to go, we can go back right now.'

Joanna hunched her shoulders. 'I—I want to go.'

'Good.'

In silence they negotiated the stile, and set off up the track which ran for some distance beside snow-banked hedges. It was exhausting walking, but exhilarating in the keen air, and Joanna's hands and feet were soon tingling with warmth, her cheeks rosy red.

At the top of the rise, they looked down on a shallow hollow where more than a dozen relics of Celtic occupation formed a ragged circle. The wind whistled eerily between these ancient monoliths, and as they approached Joanna wondered, as she had done on many occasions, how those early settlers had succeeded in erecting them. The tallest of the group was almost twenty feet in height, and yet they stood through all the seasons of the year, immune to the elements, a relic of times before Christ walked the earth.

Shannon took off his driving gloves, thrusting them into his pocket, and took hold of the frost-encrusted stone with his bare hands. 'This should convince you of man's mortality,' he said, turning to look at Joanna. 'We are but grains of sand, isn't that what the Bible says? And how many grains have shifted since these stones were first laid?'

Joanna bent her head. 'I don't want to talk about it.'

Shannon shrugged, walking to the middle of the circle. 'I wonder what this place was really used for? Nobody really knows. Oh, historians have their theories, but we all know how biased one man's opinion can be. Perhaps it was a place of worship, of sacrifice—or more prosaically, a

135

giant time-keeper.'

'Does it matter?' Joanna shifted restlessly. 'I don't want a lecture on ancient history.'

'What do you want, I wonder?' he murmured, and then, shedding the brooding tension which had come between them, he bent and lifted a handful of snow, shaping it into a ball and throwing it at her. It hit her sleeve, spilling over the brown material of her parka, and she looked down at it in surprise.

Then, determinedly, taking her mood from him, she took off her own mitts, stuffing them into her pockets, before gathering up some snow and returning his attack.

The battle was fast and furious. The stones made ideal hiding places, and Joanna crouched protectively behind them while she gathered her ammunition, making successful forays into the field to deliver her offensive. Shannon's aim was more effective than hers. Occasionally he caught her squarely in the chest and that hurt. But mostly he tempered his ability to match hers, until she collapsed into helpless giggles when one particularly accurate missile hit his cheek and sprayed snow down the neck of his parka.

'I'll get you for that!' he shouted in threatening tones, and she squealed in alarm as he began to advance steadily towards her.

Turning, she ran off through the snow, not really caring where she was going, laughing and stumbling as he came after her. She trod carelessly as she ran, twisting her ankles heedlessly, intent only on escape. He threw one snowball after her, and it hit her bruisingly in the small of her back. She could hear him overtaking her, the sound of his quickened breathing coming inevitably closer, and taking too big a stride she lost her balance, and tumbled ignominiously into the snow at his feet. It was frozen, and crunched beneath her weight, and she lay there helplessly, laughingly covering her face when he came to stand over her.

He didn't speak, and after a moment she slowly took her

136

hands away, her breath catching at the expression on his face.

'Get up, Joanna,' he muttered harshly, but for once she did not obey him.

'Help me,' she said, her voice very low, holding out her hands.

He bent to pull her up, but she resisted, and the jerk she gave on his wrists overbalanced him, so that he fell beside her, his body half covering hers. His weight was a sensuous pleasure, the stirring hardness of his body a betrayal she had long awaited. He looked down into her face, now only inches away from his, and his eyes lingered on the parted softness of her mouth.

'Do you know what you're doing?' he demanded thickly, one hand curving about her neck, his thumb probing the hollows below her jawline.

Joanna's breathing was quick and shallow. 'Does it matter?' she cried desperately, unable to control the demands within her.

'Yes, it matters,' he told her, a pulse jerking near his temple. 'God, Joanna, you don't know—you can't know, and yet——' He broke off, shaking his head vigorously. 'Oh, God, you make it so difficult for me!'

'I love you, Shannon,' she breathed impulsively. 'I do. I know I do. I think I always have. I know you're going to tell me it's no use—that we're related——'

'We're *not* related!' he told her savagely. 'My God, you don't suppose I'd allow myself—that I'd allow you——'

But Joanna interrupted him, her speech barely coherent as a surging rush of agony and ecstasy engulfed her. 'Wh-what?' she gulped. 'What did you—say? Shannon, what—what was it? What did you mean? We—we're not—not related?'

'Calm down, calm down,' he muttered, dragging himself away from her, getting to his feet as she struggled up, shaking the snow from his clothes. 'Joanna, I—I shouldn't have said that.'

'But you did, you did. You did say it,' she cried, facing him, her eyes wide and anxious. 'Shannon—Shannon, please. Tell me what you meant? You must tell me!'

'Must I?'

She was chilled by the look in his eyes as he stared down at her for a long, disturbing moment. Then, turning, he strode away towards the circle of stones, stamping the snow from his legs as he went. Joanna stared after him, her lips forming his name soundlessly, then she too stumbled after him, trying to catch up with his exhausting strides.

When he reached the circle of stones he halted, looking up towards the lowering skies through narrowed eyes, his expression hard and brooding, as if he despised the weakness he had shown. Joanna watched him helplessly, moving her shoulders in a gesture almost of defeat, and he turned his head to look at her.

His back was against one of the broader boulders, his feet slightly apart as he rested there, his dark hair made unruly by the wind. Joanna's hood had fallen back in their struggles, and long strands of honey-blonde hair framed her face with a silken curtain. Long slender legs, encased to the knee in warm boots, were visible below the hem of the thick parka, which concealed the curving contours of her body, and as she stood there she was conscious of his intent gaze taking in every detail of her appearance. Her hands moved almost defensively to smooth her hair behind her ears, but were arrested by him saying: 'Come here.'

On trembling legs she approached him, moving slowly and uncertainly, painfully aware of the power he had to hurt her. As she neared him, he put up his hand and unzipped his heavy jacket, drawing her attention to the lean strength of his body. When she halted in front of him, her breathing was hard and laboured, as if she had been running a strenuous race instead of crossing a few yards of snow-covered turf.

138

'Shannon——' she began, but he shook his head silently, his manner violent and impatient.

Then, almost against his will, she thought, he reached out and unzipped her parka, a controlled, yet savage, gesture, that brought a gasp of surprise from her lips. His hands went inside the opened jacket, closing on her hips and drawing her irrevocably towards him. She yielded against him willingly, her thighs intimately moulded to his, able to feel every hardening muscle of his taut body.

And still he didn't speak, he just held her there, the long lashes narrowing his eyes to slits. Then his hands slid behind her back, under the woollen jersey she was wearing, seeking the warm softness of her skin. The movement brought her closer, and he bent his head and trailed his lips along the side of her neck.

'Oh, Joanna,' he muttered wearily, his face tormented. 'I knew I shouldn't have come back here. But, dear God! why shouldn't I have something to remember ...'

And with a muffled groan, his mouth took possession of hers with an urgency that sent the blood pounding madly through her head. For Joanna, who until recently had believed herself capable of controlling her feelings, it was a devastating assault on her emotions, and she was hardly aware of anything in those few moments but a desire to satisfy his needs and her own. His mouth devoured hers, parting her lips, filling her with the scent and feel of his masculinity, setting her senses clamouring. His hands moved caressingly over her back, arousing sensual sensations she had not even known existed inside her, weakening her legs and making her ache with the longing for something she had never before experienced.

'Does Philip Lawson touch you like this?' he demanded, in a strangled tone, and then, before she could speak, shook his head derisively. 'No—don't answer that. I have no right to ask.'

'You do, you do,' she protested, her hands sliding up his

139

chest to his face, touching his lips and probing the hollows of his ears. 'You must know, no one has ever been this close to me. Oh, Shannon, you love me, don't you? Say you do! I don't care about anything else. I just want to hear you say it!'

Her words seemed to bring him to his senses, but it was with obvious reluctance that he pushed her away from him, his face twisting almost in self-disgust as he reached for the zip of his parka.

'Don't ask me that, Joanna!' he told her harshly. 'I can't answer you. I have no right to involve you in my miserable existence.'

'But I want to be involved! Shannon——' The pain of his words was that much more shocking because she had been unprepared for it. 'You—you said we were not related. Why shouldn't you tell me you love me?'

'Perhaps—because I don't,' he answered cruelly, and then relented when he saw the stricken spasm that crossed her face. 'Oh, God, all right, Joanna—I love you. But it's no use. It never was, and it never will be. You might as well be my sister for all the good I can do you.'

Joanna gasped. 'I—I don't believe that. If we're not related——'

'There are other considerations,' he muttered, straightening away from the pillar. 'And I've already said too much.'

'You can't mean that. I have to know about us, Shannon. How—how are we not—not related?'

'I can't tell you that.'

'But you must!'

'There's no "must" about it. We've had these moments, Joanna. Without fear of retribution. But that's as far as I'm prepared to go.'

Joanna spread her hands frustratedly. 'But why? *Why?* Surely I have a right to know who—who our parents are.'

Shannon raked a hand through his hair. 'Leave it, Joanna.'

'I—I'll ask Daddy.'

'Do you want to kill him?' Shannon was coldly matter-of-fact.

'I don't understand . . .'

'Your father's a proud man, Joanna. How do you think he'll feel if you tell him you have doubts about your relationship? He's far from recovered. Can you take the risk that might push him over the brink?'

'Then—then Mummy——'

'Your mother knows nothing.' Shannon shrugged. 'And I doubt you'd get the truth from your father. It's old history, Joanna. Best forgotten.'

'How can you say that?'

Shannon's mouth tightened. 'I've been saying it for ten years, Joanna!' He turned away. 'Oh, come on! Let's get back to the Rover. I'm frozen now.'

He walked away and Joanna stared after him disbelievingly. She didn't know what to think. Those moments in Shannon's arms had made coherent thought difficult, and while she had to accept what he said, it was hard to believe that it made no difference to him. How could he say he loved her in one breath and then deny any chance of a future together in another? And how could they not be related? If her mother knew nothing about it? It didn't make sense.

Seated in the Range Rover, she kept strictly to her own side of the vehicle, ignoring the attempts he made to restore their association to its former footing by talking about the weather and the state of the roads. She was bewildered and confused, her emotions bruised and vulnerable, but as she sat there, one thing became clear to her: if her mother knew nothing about the situation, Shannon must not be her father's son. That was the only solution. But how could that be? Maxwell Carne had not divorced his first wife until Shannon was almost six years old. Knowing the kind of man her father was, she knew with insight that if he had known Shannon was not his son, he would have done something about it before then. Unless he had not known . . .

They were bouncing over the frozen ruts in the road, and Shannon needed all his concentration to keep the Range Rover from skidding. Looking sideways at him, Joanna felt a hopeless sense of longing. She loved him so much, it was incredible to think that for ten years she had been waiting for this. And now it was to be taken away from her again. She could not allow that to happen.

'Who was your father, Shannon?' she asked softly, and was rewarded by the angry glance he cast in her direction. 'I'm not an idiot, Shannon,' she went on steadily. 'I do have powers of calculation. It stands to reason that if my mother's not involved, yours must be.'

Shannon stood on the brakes, bringing the heavy vehicle to a halt in the cleared entry to the track of a farmhouse. Then he turned sideways in his seat towards her, but his expression was not encouraging.

'All right,' he said, through tight lips. 'Having gone so far, I realise I must go further. But what I'm about to tell you will make no difference to our relationship, do you understand?'

Joanna pressed her knees together, but she made no comment, and he flung himself back in his seat, reaching moodily for the cheroots he occasionally smoked.

'You'll have guessed that my mother was pregnant before she married your father,' he told her bitterly. 'Naturally, Maxwell Carne had no idea, and Jacqueline took good care he didn't suspect . . .' He paused to light the long narrow cigar he had placed between his teeth. 'And of course, when I was born, he was delighted. He had wanted a son, and I was strong and healthy. Exactly the kind of child to satisfy his ego. And Jacqueline allowed that—for a while.'

'She told him?' Joanna was horrified.

'Ultimately. But not before she had some other man lined up. Then, when your father refused to divorce her, she explained the facts of life.'

'Oh, Shannon!'

He inhaled deeply on his cheroot. 'It's a common enough story, at least today it is. In those days, it was rather less publicised.'

'So—so did she want to take you away with her?'

Shannon's laugh was short and mirthless. 'Oh, God, no! What would Jacqueline want with a kid not yet into the schoolroom? No, she just wanted her freedom, so she threatened to tell everyone that I was not Maxwell's child. You can imagine the reaction.'

Joanna nodded, filled with compassion for the child he had been, the innocent scapegoat for his mother's faults.

He sighed. 'Of course, I knew nothing about it then. I knew my mother was unhappy—discontented. That she had terrible rows with the man I believed to be my father. I had no idea why.' He wound down his window and flicked ash outside. 'Anyway, eventually pride got the better of Maxwell Carne. It was better to be the innocent party to a divorce case than the outraged parent of a bastard child!'

'Shannon, you're not a—a——'

'Go on, say it. I've heard it used against me many times since then.'

'From—from Daddy?'

Shannon bent his head. 'Forget it.' He exhaled a cloud of tobacco smoke. 'Afterwards, as you know, Maxwell married your mother. I didn't really notice any difference in his attitude to me. I missed my mother for a while, but we had never been really close, she saw to that, and your mother was very kind to me. Then you were born.'

Joanna watched him anxiously. 'Did that make a difference?'

'Not immediately. I think your father was disappointed you weren't a boy. But he expected better next time. Unfortunately, as you know, there was no next time.'

Joanna shook her head. 'So how did you find out?'

143

Shannon hunched his shoulders. 'Can't you just take it that I did?'

'Please.'

He moved restlessly, his thigh brushing hers. 'I guess I was about sixteen at the time. You were eight—and—well, your father became jealous of our relationship.' He paused, obviously finding this a painful recollection. 'You were quite a precocious infant, and we used to spend a lot of time together.'

'I know. I remember.'

'Yes, well—if you remember, I taught you to swim, in the river. We used to go swimming quite a lot, and the day your father came on us, I was endeavouring to teach you artificial respiration.' His face twisted into a grimace. 'God knows what he thought we were doing!' He took a deep breath. 'He sent you back to the house, said something about your mother, looking for you. Then he—took his belt to me.'

'Oh, Shannon!'

Shannon's nostrils thinned. 'Don't look like that. I could stand it. It was what he said that sickened me.'

Joanna nodded. 'And then?'

He shrugged. 'You could say that everything went on as before. And to a certain extent it did. But I had changed— not least, towards you.'

'But you went away!' she cried.

'Eventually, yes.'

'Why?'

Shannon sounded bitterly amused. 'Need you ask?'

'But why could you—why couldn't we——?'

'Once I knew I was not your father's son, I took an aversion to everything that reminded me of him. Until then, I had intended going to agricultural college, learning to manage the estate. But instead, as you know, I took engineering as my subject.'

'Even so . . .'

144

'When I came back from university, I went to see your father and told him my feelings for you.' His fists clenched. 'God, he practically went insane! We had a terrible row.' He licked his lips. 'He told me there was no earthly chance of our ever meaning anything to one another, that he'd kill me before he allowed the truth of what Jacqueline had done to get out. As I keep telling you, Joanna, your father's pride is an overwhelming thing. He meant what he said. And you were only a kid. How could I be sure you'd grow up to feel the same way I did? And I owed your father everything. I knew I had no right to ask you to choose between us.'

'But you *did*!'

'No.' He shook his head.

'But Daddy wants you to have the estate now.'

'I know. And I don't want it.'

Joanna moved her head in a confused gesture. 'Why is he so eager?' She paused. 'That's why you said he didn't have to buy your silence. Do you think that's what he's trying to do?'

'I don't know. I haven't figured it out yet. Maybe coming so close to death made him realise his own mortality. Who would take over if anything happened to him? Who would care for your mother? He knew she couldn't take care of herself, that I wouldn't desert her. She was always kind to me.'

'And she really doesn't know that you're—that you're not——'

'—your father's offspring? No. No one does, I've told you. He swore he'd kill me if I breathed a word to a living soul. And now I've told you.'

Joanna's lips trembled. 'I made you.'

Shannon shook his head. 'No, you didn't. You're not to blame. I was selfish enough to want something to remember for the rest of my life.' His eyes sought hers. 'You gave me that, at least.'

'Shannon, I want to give you everything!' she breathed.

145

'No.' He swung abruptly round in his seat, squashing out the remains of his cheroot in the ashtray before turning the ignition. 'If you do anything to alter the situation, I shall leave immediately. I mean that. Your father may have his faults, but he was not to blame for what my mother did——'

'Nor were you!'

'That's as maybe. It's fruitless to argue about who's to blame. The facts of the matter are these—to all intents and purposes, we are half-brother and sister. To attempt to change any of that would succeed where that stroke your father had did not. I've spoken to his doctor. With reasonable care, there's no reason why he shouldn't live for many more years. Can you take that away from him? Can you build your own life on the destruction of another's?'

'That's not fair!'

Shannon made a harsh sound in his throat. 'Do you think I don't know that?'

Joanna pressed her palms together. 'But there has to be something we can do!'

'No, Joanna.' He swung the heavy vehicle back on to the road, switching on the sidelights as the gloom of late afternoon cast shadows across the way ahead.

'But I can't marry—Philip. Not now!'

Shannon's fingers tightened on the wheel. 'That's for you to decide. Don't talk to me about it. It's not my concern.'

Joanna caught her breath back on a sob. 'You really don't care, do you? You're so—so cool!'

Shannon uttered an oath, his foot increasing its pressure on the accelerater. 'Oh, yes,' he muttered savagely, 'I'm cool, aren't I? So cool that I can't even contemplate the idea of you marrying anyone, let alone that—that—*Philip*!'

'What—what about you? What does that woman—Camilla—mean to you?'

'Camilla?' Shannon's smile was bitter. 'Camilla restored my faith in human nature, do you know that? She gave me sanity, when all around me had gone mad!'

'You—care for her?'

He glanced sideways at her. 'I care *about* her. She's had a raw deal, too. She and her brother came up from the Transvaal with me and Brad.' He braked for a bend. 'We were all misfits together.'

Joanna looked down at her hands. 'Will you—when you get back to Kwyana, will you——'

She couldn't finish, and Shannon ground his teeth together, swinging the car off the road so violently that they almost overturned in the ditch. Then he reached for her, dragging her roughly into his arms, and covering her mouth with his own. If anything, it was more demanding than before, and Joanna moaned beneath the probing possession of his hands.

'You see what's going to happen if I stay here?' he muttered into her neck. 'I want you already, and God help me, I don't know how long I can prevent myself from taking what you're offering.' Her parka was unfastened, and his hands slid beneath her sweater, caressing the pointed swell of her breasts. 'Oh, Joanna, I love you, I love you, but you've got to stay away from me—stop tormenting me! You know what you're doing to me—you can feel it! Don't you realise, I could make you pregnant! This is madness!'

'Is it?' she breathed, all glowing woman as she wound her arms around his neck, and his groan of protest was lost in the hunger of his kiss.

The sound of someone tapping on Shannon's window made him drag himself away from her, and she straightened her clothes with trembling fingers while he rolled down the condensation-covered pane.

'Had an accident, have you? Can I help——' began a voice Joanna recognised only too well. 'My God, it's you!' Ben Lawson spoke contemptuously. 'I didn't realise. I didn't recognise the Rover in the dark.' He slapped his hand against the bonnet. 'Well, aren't you the dark horse?'

'Get out of here, Lawson.'

147

Shannon's voice was cool and controlled, but when he wound his window up again, Ben Lawson's hand prevented him, and bending, he looked into the car.

'Come on, introduce me to your girl-friend!' he jibed, but as his eyes accustomed themselves to the gloom and he recognised the girl beside the other man, he fell back a step, aghast. 'My God!' he gulped. 'Joanna! Why, you—you filthy little——'

He would have stumbled back to his Land-Rover parked just behind them then, but before he could regain his balance, Shannon had shot out of the Range Rover and had him by the lapels of his coat.

'You keep a civil tongue in your head, Lawson!' he snapped savagely, threateningly. 'And you keep what you've seen here to yourself, understand?'

Ben struggled to free himself, but although he was a broader man, he was not as strong, and Shannon held him without visible effort. Nevertheless, he wasn't finished yet. 'How're you going to make me, Carne?' he jeered scornfully. 'I'm not afraid of you!'

'No?' Shannon tightened his grip so that the hot colour was convulsed in Lawson's face.

Joanna was horrified. She slid across the seats, crying: 'Shannon—you'll choke him!' but he ignored her.

'You listen to me, Lawson,' he told the other man grimly, and Lawson had no choice but to listen, his mouth opening and shutting like a speared fish.

'What are you doing?' Mrs Lawson's voice was shrill and panic-stricken, and Joanna sank down in the driving seat, feeling an agony of responsibility for all this. Philip's mother ran wildly towards her husband and Shannon, grabbing Shannon's arms and trying to pull him away. 'Let go of him! You're mad, can't you see you're strangling him?'

Shannon shook her off, concentrating his attention on Philip's father. 'You spill one word of this to anyone, and

I'll make sure you end up in a prison cell! Do you understand me? That is—if I don't spill you myself!'

'Get your hands off him!' Mrs Lawson looked round desperately and saw Joanna kneeling on Shannon's seat. 'What are you thinking of, you stupid girl! Stop him! Stop him! He's killing him!'

Joanna thrust open the door and scrambled out, but Shannon had let Lawson go by now, and he was standing rubbing defensive hands over the bruised skin of his neck. Joanna halted hesitantly, and Philip's father turned burning eyes on her.

'You—you——' he began, but a look from Shannon silenced him.

Mrs Lawson was beside her husband, taking his arm anxiously, looking up into his blotchy face. 'Are you all right, Ben?'

Shannon pushed Joanna towards the Range Rover, and after a moment's hesitation she climbed back inside. But Mrs Lawson wasn't finished yet.

'Selfish little bitch!' she muttered. Then: 'You needn't think you've got away with this, Shannon Carne. Attacking an innocent man for no reason. We only stopped because we thought someone had got into difficulties.'

'And instead you got into them yourselves,' retorted Shannon laconically. 'And your husband is no innocent, Mrs Lawson. Believe me, he knows exactly what I'm talking about.'

'You—you can't threaten decent people, Carne,' growled her husband, regaining a little of his courage with her approval. 'You haven't heard the last of this.'

'I hope I have,' said Shannon, his eyes narrowed, and Joanna thought if he ever looked at her like that she would die. 'I really hope I have. I meant what I said, Lawson. I may have more to lose than you, but if you speak one word of what you think you've seen, I'll be looking for you.'

Lawson tried to square his shoulders and stick out his

chin, but it was a hollow gesture and they both knew it. Without another word, he turned and staggered to the Land-Rover, Mrs Lawson scolding him as they went, unaware of the real reasons behind the confrontation she had just witnessed.

Joanna was shaking like a leaf when Shannon got back behind the wheel, slamming the door behind him with suppressed violence. Then he expelled his breath on a long sigh, and bent forward to rest his forehead against the coldness of the steering wheel.

'I'm sorry.' Joanna didn't know what else to say, and she had to say something. 'I'm sorry.'

'Why?' he demanded in a muffled voice. 'It wasn't your fault.'

'How can you say that? Ben Lawson——'

'—will say nothing.'

'You can't be sure of that. I don't like that man, I never have. Why did you threaten him? What do you know that I don't?'

Shannon lifted his head and flicked back his cuff. 'Do you realise it's after four? Your parents will be wondering what I'm doing with you.'

'Shannon! You didn't answer me.'

He sighed. 'Let's just say—the yield from the herd was—less than usual during the weeks at High Stoop.'

'But everyone knows that cattle yield less milk at this time of the year!'

'Yes,' Shannon nodded. 'You could be right.'

He reached for the ignition, but her fingers stayed him. 'You don't believe that, do you?'

Shannon released himself and started the engine. 'Let's just say there's room for doubt.'

'Was that why Daddy wanted the herd back again?'

'Your mother was responsible for allowing Lawson to take them. Your father would never have let them go. He didn't trust Lawson, and nor do I.'

Joanna looked at his profile with a sense of desperation. 'Oh, Shannon, what am I going to do?'

'You're going to do exactly what you would have done before. Go on living in Mallowsdale, while I go back to Kwyana.'

'I can't ...'

'You must.' He stretched out a hand and covered both of hers where they lay in her lap. 'Don't make it any harder for either of us, Joanna. We've had today. Let's just remember it as a day out of time.'

CHAPTER ELEVEN

JOANNA knelt on the window seat in the library, watching anxiously for the Range Rover as darkness closed about the Hall. Shannon should have been home by now. He had left for Carlisle before nine o'clock that morning, and it was already after five. He had never been so late. Where was he? What could he be doing?

She rubbed away the condensation on the glass caused by her own breath, and as she did so, she saw the circle of whiteness on her finger left by Philip's engagement ring. She had given up wearing the ring, but as yet she had not been able to bring herself to tell him that she was not going to marry him. Since Shannon's confrontation with his father, he had been especially nice to her, had even made an effort to be polite to Shannon himself, and Joanna had been unable to find it in her heart to shatter his confidence. But she would have to tell him. That much she knew. And the longer she put it off, the harder it would get.

It was three weeks since that day she and Shannon had gone to Penrith, and since then Shannon had taken good care never to be alone with her. She guessed he must know how he was hurting her—hurting them both—but he was succeeding in convincing her that there could be no future for them.

Joanna's health had suffered in consequence, and perhaps that was why Philip had been so gentle with her, that and the arrival of the new manager. Matthew Price was a man in his late thirties, widowed and not unattractive, towards whom Maxwell Carne had taken an immediate liking. His presence at the Hall—Joanna's mother had suggested he should stay with them until one of the cottages on the estate could be made habitable for him—had probably made Philip and his parents realise that he and Joanna were not married yet. That plans could go astray. And Joanna was cynical enough to appreciate that whatever she was, whatever she had done, in the Lawsons' eyes, she was still Maxwell Carne's daughter.

'Close the curtains, Joanna.'

Her father's voice behind her made her realise that her vigil had not gone unobserved, and although she wanted to refuse, she stepped obediently down from the seat and drew the heavy velvet curtains against the darkness outside. Then she walked restlessly across the room, stopping beside her father's wheelchair to say:

'Is there anything you want before I go and see if Mummy wants any help?'

Maxwell Carne looked up at her steadily. 'He's not coming back, Joanna,' he said heavily, and while a wave of cold sickness swept over her she guessed what it had cost him to say that. Even so, she could not accept it.

'Not yet,' she agreed quickly, moving towards the door, but he stopped her.

'You know what I mean,' he insisted. 'Shannon's not coming back to Mallowsdale. Not tonight. Not ever.'

Joanna had to grasp a chair to support herself. 'I—I don't understand . . .'

'I think you do, Joanna. Shannon's gone. Back to Kwyana.' His eyes moved to the clock on the mantel. 'His flight was due to leave Heathrow an hour ago.'

Joanna closed her eyes against the actual agony which engulfed her. He was gone! Shannon was gone! Without even saying goodbye. And her father had known . . .

Not trusting herself to speak, she made her way on trembling legs to the door, only stopping when her father swung his chair round and said: 'Pull yourself together, girl! I wouldn't indulge myself as you do. He's gone. You knew he would be going, sooner or later, and Price has

153

proved to be a perfectly satisfactory substitute.'

Joanna opened her mouth, but for a moment no words would come. Then she swallowed convulsively, and said chokingly: 'That's all you care about, isn't it? So long as the estate doesn't suffer!'

'What else is there for me to care about?' demanded her father harshly. His eyes narrowed. 'And what's it to you anyway? You're getting married in three months. You'll have your own life to live. What happens here won't concern you.'

Joanna moved her head from side to side with slow persistence. 'No. *No.* I—shan't be getting married——'

'What do you mean?' Maxwell's heavy brows ascended.

'Just—what I say. I'm—not going to marry Philip.'

'Why not?'

She was tempted to tell him, she was *so* tempted. That he could have remained silent all day, knowing Shannon was not coming back, not giving her the chance to telephone him at the airport even, to hear his voice just one more time . . .

But that must have been Shannon's decision, she reasoned, with reluctant honesty. It was exactly the sort of thing he would do. He knew better than she how devastating farewells could be. Tears stung the back of her eyes. It had been bad enough before, knowing he was soon leaving, never being given the opportunity to be alone with him. But nothing could compare to the desolation that filled her now.

Forcing back the tears, she said unevenly: 'I—don't love him.'

Maxwell looked suspicious. 'Don't you?'

'I—no.' Joanna looked down at her hand, knuckles white as it gripped the handle of the door. 'I—I've realised for some time that—that it was no good—between us.'

Maxwell's wheelchair came irrevocably across the floor towards her. It was electrically operated, and only the whisper of its wheels heralded its progress. Joanna didn't look at her father, but his good hand came out and gripped her wrist, hard and painfully.

'Is this anything to do with Shannon?' he demanded between his teeth, his face contorted by some emotion Joanna didn't care to identify.

The pain of her wrist gave her a reason for her tears, but she tore her hand away and exclaimed: 'How—how could it be?'

Maxwell's whole body sagged, and the features of his face relaxed abruptly. 'I don't know,' he muttered, but with relief she knew he had accepted what she said. He turned his chair about and returned to his former position on the hearth. 'That boy's been nothing but trouble to me!' he continued, in low resentful tones.

Joanna could not listen to that. Dear God, that he could actually convince himself of what he was saying when——

She swung open the door, supporting herself against the jamb. 'I'll see you later,' she got out jerkily, and somehow she was outside and the door was closed behind her.

She stumbled across the hall to the stairs as body-shaking sobs rose helplessly into her throat, and sank down weakly on to the lower treads. She couldn't move, she was racked with misery, and eventually her mother found her there and had to fetch Henry Barnes to help her get the girl upstairs.

For three days Joana didn't leave her bed, and the incidence of a mild cold gave her mother an excuse to call the doctor and have him examine her without arousing comment.

'Well, young lady,' Doctor Stewart said cajolingly, folding his stethoscope back into his case, 'this is no way to treat yourself. Lying here, indulging in futile emotion.' Her mother had left them alone, and he seated himself on the side of her bed and looked down at her curiously. 'Can't you be thankful you're healthy? There are dozens of young people *forced* to spend their days in bed. They'd give

155

anything to have your opportunities.'

Joanna nodded uncomfortably. 'I—I'm all right.'

'No, you're not. Or I wouldn't be here.'

'Mummy thinks my cold isn't getting better.'

'Does she?' The elderly doctor regarded her doubtfully. He had been present at her birth in this very house, and he did not need his medical training to see that there was more than a cold troubling her. 'What is it, Joanna? Having trouble with that boy-friend of yours?'

'*No!*' Joanna turned her face away from him. 'I've told you—I'm fine. Mummy wasted your time bringing you here.'

'I don't think so.' He paused. 'Shannon's gone back to Africa, I hear.' Joanna nodded, her lips tightening, and he went on: 'Nice boy, Shannon. I always liked him.'

Almost reluctantly, Joanna found her eyes turning back to him. 'Did—did you know—his mother?'

Doctor Stewart hesitated. Then he nodded. 'Yes, of course I knew her.'

Joanna's lips parted. Showing more animation than she had shown for days, she propped herself up on her elbows, staring at him intently. 'Were—were you here when— Shannon was born?'

The doctor sighed. 'Yes. But what——'

Joanna shook her head, sinking back against the pillows, her brow furrowed. 'I—I was curious, that's all,' she said.

Doctor Stewart got up from the bed. 'Well, I must be going. I have other patients to attend to.'

Joanna watched him anxiously. 'I'm sorry if I've wasted your time.'

'You'll only have wasted my time if you don't show some improvement,' he told her shortly. 'Get out of that bed! Get dressed! Start living again. How do you think Shannon would feel if he knew what you were doing to yourself?'

Joanna gasped. 'Shannon?'

'I'm not completely without perception, Joanna,' Doctor

Stewart replied, walking towards the door. 'I'll leave a prescription for some capsules with your mother,' and opening the door he left her.

Although Doctor Stewart's visit had done little enough for her, it did serve to break through Joanna's apathy, and within a couple of days she was up and about again. The capsules he had prescribed ensured her a decent night's sleep at least, and during the day she had to cope with her shredded emotions.

Philip came over to the house one evening towards the end of the week and found her looking almost recovered, pale and ethereal-looking in a long soft woollen gown of palest blue, her hair loose about her shoulders. He thought she had never looked more beautiful, and he was absolutely stunned when after a few brief words of greeting, she handed him back his ring.

'I'm sorry, Philip,' she said, lifting her slim shoulders in a helpless gesture of dismissal, 'but I don't love you. I thought I did—but I was mistaken.'

Philip sank down weakly on to a low couch set before the log fire that burned here in the small sitting room at the Hall. For a few minutes he was too shocked to say anything, but gradually, as her words sank in, a feeling of angry indignation gripped him.

'But you can't do this to me!' he blustered. 'Everything's arranged! Mum and Dad are moving out in June, and we're taking over!'

Joanna sighed. She had known it would not be easy. 'I'm sorry, Philip,' she said again. 'I know I'm letting you down badly, but better now than later.'

'What do you mean?'

'I—we might have got married, and afterwards . . .'

'That's nonsense!' Philip wasn't having that. 'Once we were married, you'd be too busy taking care of me and the farm to even think about anyone else, if that's what you're

157

implying. Besides, there'd be babies . . .'

'Well—perhaps,' she conceded quietly. 'But anyway, this way is better. I know now it would never have worked. You and me. I just—I didn't know. I didn't have any experience. I had nothing to judge our relationship against.'

'And now you have?' he demanded offensively.

Joanna flushed. 'That's my business.'

'Damn you, is it? By God, you're a cool one,' he muttered angrily. 'The chap's only been in the district three weeks, but your father's already been able to persuade you that he's a better proposition!'

'I don't know——'

'Don't give me that. What's your father told you? That now that Shannon's thrown in his hand, he's prepared to make the estate over to you, providing you marry the man of *his* choice?'

'Philip!'

'Oh, I've seen it coming. Ever since that smarmy-mouthed individual set foot in Mallowsdale. Damned scrounger. Managing this estate, and acting like he owned the b——'

'Philip! If you're talking about Matt——'

'Oh, *Matt*, is it?' Philip snorted furiously. 'And you think you can throw me over for him? Some mealy-mouthed Southerner!'

'Philip, please . . .'

But even as she said the words, Joanna felt a sense of relief. Why not let Philip think there was something between her and Matthew Price? He'd soon be proved wrong, but at least it would take the emphasis away from Shannon.

'Well, I won't let you do this, Joanna!' he told her savagely, getting up from the couch and taking her by the shoulders. 'You're my fiancée, and you're staying that way. I won't let you go.' And his soft lips fastened themselves to hers, revolting her utterly when all she wanted to remember was the urgent pressure of Shannon's hard mouth.

158

She struggled to free herself, beating at him with her small fists, but he would not let her go, and she made desperate sounds of fury as he continued to kiss her. Then the door behind them opened, and a quiet, cultivated voice said: 'Oh, I'm sorry. I thought this room was empty.'

Philip lifted his head at the interruption, and Joanna seized on the momentary respite to cry: 'Matt! Matt! Don't go!' in hoarse, appealing tones.

'Joanna?' Ignoring Philip's rude demand that he should leave them, Matthew Price came further into the room. 'Do you want me, Joanna?'

She nodded vigorously, and at last her pressure on Philip's chest had some effect, and he let her go. She put the width of the couch between them, and putting up a trembling hand to her tumbled hair, looked gratefully at Matthew.

'Thank you,' she said. 'I—Philip was just leaving, weren't you, Philip?'

There was an awful moment when she thought Philip intended making a fight of it. But he was more like his father than she had thought. Muttering bitterly to himself, he marched across the room, and a few moments later they heard the front door slam behind him. Only then did Joanna sink down wearily on to the arm of a chair, putting both hands to her throat.

'I'm sorry about that, Matt,' she apologised, glancing up at the new manager, standing regarding her with some concern. 'I—we—I've just broken my engagement.'

'I see.' Matthew nodded understandingly. 'No wonder Lawson looked so furious. I think I'd have felt the same in the circumstances.'

Joanna half smiled. 'Thank you.'

Matthew's colour deepened. For all he had been married, he was still rather a shy man, and she had found she could embarrass him quite easily. While Shannon was still in the house, she had used him deliberately in an effort to make

159

Shannon jealous, and now she realised how selfish she had been to try such a thing, for all their sakes. He was an attractive man, too, above medium height with pleasant, even features and brown hair. He was the kind of man she knew instinctively would never hurt her, a man she could rely on. Perhaps she ought to consider marrying someone like him, she thought bitterly. She could, at least, be sure that he would make no demands on her she was not prepared to fulfil.

Or would he? Dejection overwhelmed her. What was the point of pretending? Matthew was nice, he was kind, he would make a good husband—but he was a man. He would want a wife in every sense of the word, and that was something she could not contemplate with any man but Shannon. In that little time they had had together, she had learned what it was to want a man, to desire and need him, until she had ached with longings that had not been assuaged. How could she even consider such intimacies with anyone else, when even thinking about Shannon turned her limbs to water?

'Are you all right? He didn't hurt you, did he?'

Matthew's solicitude was a soothing balm, and she looked up at him with warm gratitude. 'No, I'm all right,' she reassured him quickly. 'And I should apologise for Philip, too. He's not usually so—so boorish.'

'There's no need to apologise, really,' he exclaimed, a smile lightening his rather serious expression. 'I'm just glad I was around to give my assistance.'

'Oh, so am I!' Joanna was fervent in her agreement. 'Er—won't you sit down for a while? You did come in here for that purpose, didn't you?'

'Well, yes.' He shifted uncomfortably. 'If you're sure I'm not intruding . . .'

'Heavens, no.' Joanna would be glad of his company. 'We can have the television on, if you like.' She indicated the set in the corner. 'Do you watch much television, Matt?'

160

'Not a lot,' he admitted. 'I usually read.'

'What do you like reading?'

Joanna assumed an interest, and when her mother looked into the room about half an hour later, she looked pleased to see they were getting along so well.

'Was that Philip who slammed out a little while ago?' she asked, raising her eyebrows at her daughter.

'Yes,' Joanna nodded. 'I told him.'

She had already informed her mother that the wedding was off, but Catherine had not really taken her seriously. Now, however, she showed her surprise.

'You really went through with it!' She shook her head. 'Philip won't like that, Joanna. You can't turn him off and on like a tap, you know.'

'I wouldn't dream of it,' replied Joanna calmly. 'You're stuck with me, I'm afraid.'

Her mother shook her head a trifle bewilderedly, and withdrew. Joanna guessed she would ·go and discuss the matter with her father. Thank goodness she had already told him. That was one hurdle she would not have liked to have to face again.

During the next few weeks, life resumed a certain pattern for Joanna. Now that she did not have her coming marriage to Philip to plan for, she had time to consider her future, and with a determination she had learned from Shannon, she decided to find an occupation for herself.

But it was not so easy as she had at first imagined. Her academic qualifications had been good when she left school six years ago, but convincing a would-be employer why she had never used them to any effect was another matter. Besides, there were girls, younger than she was, with just as good qualifications, attending the labour exchange every week to collect their Social Security.

But it did give her something to do, something to think about, and in her spare time, Matthew was always around to provide companionship. Maxwell was having one of the empty cottages on the estate modernised for the new manager's use, and as the evenings got lighter, Joanna often walked down to it with Matthew to see how the work was progressing. With new beams, and a modern kitchen, and central heating to keep out the draughts, the cottage was turning into a charming dwelling, and Matthew, she knew, was looking forward to having his own home again.

Then one evening in April, when the weather had been particularly mild, and Joanna had been helping Matthew to unpack some of his books into the fitted shelves at the cottage, they were interrupted by the arrival of Jessie Duxbury. She had obviously run all the way from the Hall, and her face was streaked with perspiration, her lips soft and trembling. She burst into the cottage without knocking, which was an unknown thing for her to do, and Joanna sprang to her feet, staring at her with anxious eyes. But she knew—before Jessie opened her mouth, she knew—and without waiting for explanations, she ran out of the cottage, and across the fields to the house.

She was breathless when she climbed the gate into the stableyard, and Bess, who had been chasing some chickens, gave up the game to impede her progress.

Joanna brushed the dog aside, running towards the house, and as she did so, she glimpsed the gleaming bonnet of a sleek Mercedes parked to one side of the building. But she had no time to ponder its presence, bursting into the kitchen, and through it into the hall.

It was there she encounted her mother, and Catherine Carne's face confirmed her worst fears.

'You're too late, Joanna,' she said bitterly. 'He's gone, he's gone! Your father's dead!'

Joanna looked towards the open door of the library, and as she did so a man appeared in the aperture, a tall, dark man who for a heart-stopping moment she thought was Shannon. But as he moved nearer she realised that this man was much older, greyer, yet perceptibly some relation. *His father ...?*

She dragged her gaze away from him and looked instead at her mother. Catherine gathered herself with difficulty, wiping her eyes with her handkerchief, and gesturing towards the stranger.

'This—this is Mr Steinbeck, Joanna. Er—' She looked at the man. 'This is my daughter, Joanna.'

'Hello, Joanna.'

The man was an American, and his accent was deep and attractive. Joanna allowed him to shake her hand, and then looked at her mother again.

'Mummy—what happened?'

'It's my fault, I'm afraid,' said the American quietly. 'I didn't know—Jacqueline never told me——' He broke off, and looked to Catherine for confirmation, and she nodded almost imperceptibly. 'I just wanted to see my son, Joanna. Your—brother, Shannon?'

Joanna gulped, and her mother shook her head disbelievingly 'This—this man is Shannon's father,' she said chokingly. 'And—and I never knew. Max never told me.'

Joanna hugged her mother closely, feeling suddenly protective. 'Why have you come here, Mr Steinbeck?'

The American sighed. 'I just wanted to see my son,' he said again. 'Can nobody understand that?'

The sound of a siren coming up the drive to the house brought Catherine erect. 'That will be the ambulance,' she said, through trembling lips. 'I phoned—but it's too late.'

Joanna hesitated only a moment before going to meet the ambulance men, explaining the circumstances in an undertone. The men were very kind. They accompanied her into the library, and she saw her father for the first time since his second attack. Strangely, he had a vulnerability in death he had never had in life, and the tears which until now had remained dormant stirred irresistibly.

The men examined him, and then confirmed what her

mother had said. 'There's nothing we can do,' said one of them quietly. 'Would you like us to take him upstairs—put him on a bed?'

Joanna compressed her lips. 'His room is down here. You could put him there, if you would.'

They carried Maxwell Carne on a stretcher into his bedroom, and deposited him on the bed. Then they left, and Joanna emerged from the room feeling suddenly faint. The man called Steinbeck saw the whitening of her features, and moving quickly was there to catch her when she fell.

When she opened her eyes, she was lying on the couch in the sitting room, and Matthew was standing talking to the American just inside the door. However, when they saw she was conscious, they both moved towards the couch.

'Mummy——' she began jerkily, but Matthew calmed her with a movement of his hand.

'Your mother's making some tea—with Jessie. She's all right. It's you we've been concerned about.'

Joanna struggled to get up, feeling quite a fraud. 'I—I must have fainted,' she said unsteadily. 'I'm sorry.'

'You had quite a shock,' said the American, sighing. 'What can I say? I feel this is all my doing.'

Joanna looked up at him intently. 'You're really Shannon's father?'

'Do you doubt it?'

'Oh, no.' She shook her head. 'You're very like him.' She looked at Matthew. 'Do you—I mean——'

'Yes, I know.' Matthew nodded. 'Jessie told me. Don't worry, I shan't say anything.'

'I never thought you would.' Joanna flashed him a faint smile. Then she looked again at the American. 'Tell me—why did you suddenly want to see the son you hadn't acknowledged for thirty-two years?'

Steinbeck closed his eyes for a moment. 'I didn't know I had a son, Joanna. Not until about six months ago.'

'What?'

164

'It's true. Jacqueline—that's—that's Shannon's mother—she's very ill, dying, in fact.' He paused. 'She wrote me. I guess she wanted to unburden herself before she died.'

Joanna listened in amazement. 'You mean you're not the man she's been living with?'

'Hell, no. Jacqueline and I—well, it was a wartime thing. I'm not proud of it, but it went on all the time. Sure as hell though, I didn't know she was pregnant when I went back to the States.'

Curiously enough, Joanna believed him. Jacqueline had never sounded the kind of woman to be self-sacrificing, and if she had suspected she was expecting a baby, she would have told him.

'Anyway,' he went on, 'after the war, a group of guys from my unit came back over here, looking up old places, you know the sort of thing. One of them, Bill Webster, met Jacqueline around here somewhere. He remembered her, of course. She was always a good-looking woman. By then, I guess, she was bored with being the usual housewife and mother. She wanted some excitement, and she thought Bill could give it to her. He was certainly crazy about her. She got a divorce and they came back to the States. The rest I guess you know. Except that of course I eventually met up with her again, married to Bill by this time, but just as wilful. Bill's dead now. He was killed in a plane crash a couple of years ago. Jacqueline lives alone, and maybe she's got maudlin in her old age. In any event, she wrote me, and your father, telling him what she planned to do.'

Joanna gasped. 'She wrote to Daddy? When?'

'I don't know. The end of last year, I guess. Around the same time that she wrote me.'

Joanna lay back weakly, her cheeks paling once more, and Matthew started forward. 'Joanna—what is it?'

She shook her head silently for a moment, and then she said. 'Daddy's stroke. That was towards the end of last year.'

'You don't mean——' Steinbeck uttered an oath. 'You think that's what caused your father's attack?'

'It might well have done so,' replied Joanna, putting up a hand to her throat. 'He was so afraid—so afraid . . .'

'Afraid?' Steinbeck didn't understand. 'Afraid of what?'

'Afraid that this might get out,' she explained wearily. 'Jacqueline told him, you see. That was how she got her divorce.'

Steinbeck frowned. 'You mean—you knew that Shannon was not your brother?'

She nodded. 'Shannon told me.'

'Shannon told you? You mean—he knew?'

Joanna sighed. 'It's a long story, Mr Steinbeck. But yes, Shannon knew. My father could be a—violent man.'

'I believe that.' Steinbeck moved his shoulders in a bewildered gesture. 'So everyone knew but me.'

'My mother didn't.'

'No, I gathered that. It was a terrible shock to her.' He paused. 'Even so, why all the panic? What did your father expect me to do?'

Joanna looked puzzled now. 'You mean—here—and now?'

'What harm could I do him? I only wanted to see my son, I knew I had no hold on him.'

'Did you?' Joanna could feel the tears at the backs of her eyes. She was beginning to understand so much. Shannon was more like his father than he realised. She tried to explain. 'My—my father was a possessive man, Mr Steinbeck. A jealous man, too. I don't think he could ever forget that—that Jacqueline had cheated him. So he—used Shannon as a whipping boy.'

'I see. But Shannon's not here, is he? Your mother told me he was in Lushasa, or some such place. In Africa!'

'That's right. He is. He and—and my father split up ten years ago. He was here—quite recently. After my father had his stroke, he sent for him. Shannon didn't know why.

166

Daddy—Daddy decided he wanted him to have the estate. But Shannon refused to take it.'

'Your father did that? Offered him this estate?'

'Yes. I think I know why now. He was afraid, as I've said. Afraid of you, Mr Steinbeck. He judged everybody by his own standards, I'm afraid. He would never believe that you could come here and meet Shannon without—without making your relationship known.' She stifled a slightly hysterical giggle. 'He must have been horrified when he saw you. You look so like Shannon.'

'And the estate?'

'A bribe—nothing more. A carrot, dangled before the donkey's nose to induce it to enter the tunnel. If Shannon had accepted Mallowsdale, my father would have felt—secure.'

'But that's crazy!' Steinbeck was breathing heavily. 'Surely he knew that!'

'Perhaps. There—there was one thing more.' She looked reluctantly up at Matthew, and taking the hint he nodded. 'I'll leave you alone,' he said, and left the room.

'Go on.' Steinbeck came down on the couch beside her.

Joanna bent her head, and the curtain of her hair hid her face. 'Shannon—loves me,' she murmured softly.

Steinbeck made a comprehending sound. 'Not as—his sister, I gather.'

'No.'

'Do you love him?'

'Yes. Oh, yes.'

He put out a hand and looped the nearest wing of her hair back behind her ear so that he could see her face. 'And that was bad?'

'My father was totally opposed to any kind of relationship between us. I think—I think the fact that Shannon was Jacqueline's son . . .'

Her voice trailed away, and the man beside her sighed. 'What a waste,' he muttered heavily. Then: 'Your father

167

knew that you were aware of Shannon's parentage?'

'Oh, no. No.' Joanna shook her head.

'Another reason for putting Shannon into his debt.' Steinbeck had soon absorbed the situation. 'So—what now?'

'Now?' Joanna could hardly think coherently.

'Of course.' Steinbeck studied her pale complexion. 'Joanna, the biggest obstacle to your happiness has been removed, hasn't it?'

Joanna stared at him through troubled eyes. 'Well, I— I——' She swallowed convulsively. 'Has it?'

'Well, if it helps at all, I'm prepared to state openly that Shannon is my son.'

Joanna caught her breath. 'Could you? Could you?'

'Why not? The truth is bound to come out sooner or later. No doubt a doctor——'

'A doctor! Doctor Stewart!' Joanna could feel a slow excitement stirring inside her. 'Is it possible?'

Steinbeck put his hand over hers as they lay in her lap, and she remembered the time Shannon had done that. Steinbeck's hands were even like Shannon's, brown and long-fingered, not at all like Maxwell Carne's stubby square fingers.

'You have the funeral to face first,' he said. 'Your mother needs your support. Afterwards ... Well, I'll stick around. I may be able to help.'

'You'll stay?' She looked up at him eagerly.

'If you want me to.'

'Oh, I do.' Just touching him like this brought Shannon that much nearer somehow. 'But—your wife? Your family?'

'My family are all grown up and married with families of their own,' he told her quietly. 'All except my eldest son.' He half smiled.

'And your wife?'

'My wife died last year. Just a week before I got Jacqueline's letter.'

CHAPTER TWELVE

SHANNON did not come home to see Maxwell Carne buried.

Joanna could not believe it when the day of the funeral dawned, and there had still been no word from Lushasa. He must know her father was dead, she told herself bitterly, as she waited with her mother and Henry, Matthew and Shannon's father, Andrew Steinbeck, for the hearse to arrive to take the coffin to the church in Mallowsdale. Even if he had not intended making the journey home for the funeral, he could have written or cabled, she thought despairingly, his absence making her painfully aware that so far as Shannon was concerned, her father's death altered nothing.

Andrew Steinbeck was a tower of strength, and Joanna had found herself turning more and more to him during these days of uncertainty. Her mother had become amazingly competent since the initial shock of her husband's death had subsided, and Joanna had realised with a pang that her father had been responsible for Catherine's lack of confidence. Now that she was her own woman, free to make her own decisions, she had assumed the running of the estate with an ability that shocked all of them. Except Matthew. He had become her mother's right hand, and she consulted him before making any major decisions.

Henry Barnes was leaving after the funeral. He, too, had been very kind, and his quiet personality, which for so long had been eclipsed by his employer's belligerence, had emerged during these past days.

After the funeral, there was the formality of reading the will. Martin Lewis, Maxwell Carne's solicitor, was most concerned when he discovered that Shannon was not present, which was not surprising when it was revealed that Maxwell had left everything in trust to his son, Shannon, with the stipulation that he should take care of his stepmother during her lifetime.

Joanna was hardly surprised at the revelations. She had known all along of her father's determination to make Shannon his heir. But if Shannon had suspected this, was that why he had not come back? He did not want Mallowsdale, he had made that very plain, and perhaps he had been afraid that if he came back here, he would become involved against his will. It was a destructive thought, and one which left Joanna feeling utterly shattered. Was there to be no future for them, after all? Was the hope of these last days nothing more than self-deception? She was rapidly becoming convinced that Shannon would not ever do anything to destroy the illusion of parenthood her father had created.

That evening Andrew Steinbeck came to find her while she was sitting in her father's study, idly sorting through the papers at his desk. Someone had to do it, and her mother had suggested she might like to see if there was anything she wanted to keep.

'Joanna?' Andrew came slowly into the room, but she waved him to a chair, saying: 'It's all right, I'm just poking around.'

Andrew closed the door, and then stood looking down at her rather doubtfully. In casual slacks and an open-necked shirt, he was disturbingly like Shannon, and she had to force herself to look away from him and concentrate on what she was doing.

'Joanna.' He came to stand before the desk. 'What are you going to do?'

Joanna pretended not to understand. 'What do you mean?' she asked, flicking through a sheaf of delivery notes.

'Joanna, you know very well what I mean.' He leant across the desk and took the delivery notes from her unresisting fingers. 'What are you going to do about Shannon?'

'What can I do?'

'Someone has to tell him. About the estate.'

'Don't solicitors do that sort of thing?'

'*Joanna!*' For the first time, Andrew sounded impatient with her. 'Of course the lawyers will handle it. But don't you think someone should go and see him, tell him how—how Carne died?'

Joanna shrugged. 'That's what funerals are for. If he'd been interested, he would have come.'

Andrew's fist balled against the desk. 'Stop this, Joanna. You're jumping to conclusions. There may be some reason why Shannon didn't come to the funeral. Have you thought of that?'

'What reason?'

'How should I know?' He paused. 'You have to stop torturing yourself like this, because that's what you're doing, aren't you? Are you so lacking in faith that you can't even see that there might be circumstances?'

Joanna's shoulders sagged. 'Oh, Andrew! If only I could believe that.'

'Why can't you? You told me Shannon loves you. Does love that has existed for more than ten years just *die*? I don't think so.'

Joanna's lips trembled. 'You're so good for me.'

'You should be good for yourself. Joanna, why don't you go to Lushasa? Why don't you go and see Shannon for yourself?'

Joanna bit her lip. 'Do you—do you really think I should?'

'If you still love him.'

'*If* . . .' She shook her head. 'I—I'm crazy about him.'

'So why hesitate?'

Joanna moved her shoulders bemusedly. 'I don't know. I'm afraid, I suppose. Afraid that Shannon will say this makes no difference.'

Andrew Steinbeck sounded impatient. 'If he does, then

he's a fool. A man has only one life, Joanna. He should do with it the best he can. Maxwell Carne is dead. Nothing can alter that. And memories are short, whatever people say. I should know.'

Joanna looked up at him mistily, her eyes still full of tears unshed. 'You really think I should go to Kwyana?' She hesitated. 'Would you—would you go with me?'

'Me?' Andrew Steinbeck jerked his thumb against his chest. 'I—well, are you sure?'

'Oh, yes, please!'

He frowned. 'I don't see why I shouldn't. If that's what you really want. But what will Shannon say?'

Joanna shook her head, pulling open the first drawer of the desk. 'He'll probably think he's seeing double—oh!' Her fingers had encounted a small key, pushed away in a corner of the drawer. 'I wonder what this is.'

She brought the key out, and tried it in the drawers of the desk. But it was too small for their large holes, and besides, it was made of steel and the desk locks were all brass.

'Let me have a look at it.' Andrew Steinbeck took it out of her hands. 'It looks like the key to a deed box or something. Did your father have such a thing?'

'I don't know. I don't even remember seeing it there before.' She bit her lip and got to her feet. 'I'll ask Mummy, she might know.'

Catherine Carne was in the kitchen, talking to Jessie. She frowned when Joanna showed her the key, and then nodded. 'I don't know what that is, Joanna. Your father had it on a chain round his neck. I—they gave it to me when they came to attend to your father, along with his ring. I just dropped it into a drawer. I was going to investigate it later.'

Joanna frowned. 'It must have been important, if he kept it on his person.'

'Not necessarily, Joanna. Your father was a secretive

172

man—I should know that better than anyone. He liked to have these little mysteries about him.'

Joanna sighed. 'All the same ...'

'I'm leaving now, Mrs Carne.'

Henry Barnes broke into their conversation, and on impulse Joanna turned to him, holding out the key. 'Do you know what this is, Henry?'

Henry frowned, and then his face cleared. 'Of course, I do. It's the key to that diary your father used to keep.'

'A diary?' Catherine looked astounded. 'I didn't know Max kept a diary.'

'I don't know that he did, Mrs Carne. But he always kept it with him. I didn't ever catch him writing in it, but he could have done.'

'Then where is it?' Joanna couldn't understand the rising surge of apprehension inside her.

Henry looked doubtful. 'Well, it was always with him. I should think he'd have had it in his wheelchair—when he died.'

'Did you find it?' Joanna turned to her mother, but Catherine shook her head.

'No.'

Joanna sighed. 'Is—is Daddy's chair still in the library?'

'You know it is.' Catherine bit her lower lip. 'I haven't been able to bring myself to move it yet.'

The wheelchair stood in a corner of the library, not in its usual place on the hearth, but still Joanna felt a pang as she approached it. The rug which had always covered her father's lower limbs was still thrown carelessly into it, and with trembling fingers she moved it aside. And there it was, a leather-bound five-year diary, sealed with a leather flap and locked securely.

She was aware that her mother had come to stand behind her, and on impulse she handed the key and the diary to her, indicating that she should open it. Catherine was obviously very loath to do so, but curiosity got the better of

173

her, and after a few moments of indecision she inserted the key in the lock.

The diary opened without difficulty, and looking over her mother's shoulder, Joanna saw her fingers turn to the first page. But it was empty. And so was the second, and the third. Catherine turned stricken eyes up to her daughter, and Joanna took the book from her, flicking through the pages impatiently. They were all empty, but towards the back there was something inserted between the pages, something that fluttered out as Joanna was flicking through it.

She bent and picked up the piece of paper. It was fragile after having been folded into such a small space, but the texture was still good. Together they opened it up, and Joanna found herself staring at Shannon's birth certificate.

'My God!' exclaimed Catherine, turning to stare at her daughter. 'Do you see what I see?'

Joanna saw. In the space reserved for the name of the child's father were the words—*Andrew Wilson Steinbeck*. Attached to the back of the certificate was another document which in effect changed the surname to *Carne*.

'Do you realise what this means?' whispered Catherine, in horror. 'He knew—he knew when Jacqueline had the baby that Shannon was not his child!'

'And he didn't say anything.' Joanna felt slightly sick.

'No.' Catherine pressed her lips together. 'So long as no one else knew he was prepared to keep it to himself.'

'Until Jacqueline wanted a divorce.'

'Maybe.'

'Do you think she knew he knew?'

'I shouldn't think so.' Catherine shook her head. 'Or she wouldn't have made such a big thing of it later.' She shrugged her shoulders. 'How like your father!' Her voice was bitter. 'No one ever was allowed to better him. He must have guessed as soon as the baby was born that it wasn't the premature child Jacqueline wanted him to believe.'

Joanna suddenly sank down on to the nearest chair. 'You realise what else this means, don't you?'

'What?'

'Shannon must know of the existence of this.'

'Why?'

'You need a birth certificate when you apply for a passport, don't you?'

'Heavens, yes. I didn't think of that.' Catherine made a bewildered gesture. 'And Max kept it so well hidden.'

'Am I intruding?'

Andrew Steinbeck came into the library, and Catherine gave him a rather absent smile. 'No, you're not intruding, Andrew,' she replied,–rather heavily. 'I—er—we've just found Shannon's birth certificate. I—your name's on it.'

'*What?* Let me see that.'

Andrew almost snatched the certificate out of her hands and stared at it disbelievingly. Then he looked up, and his eyes alighted on Joanna's pale face.

'Well!' he muttered, and there was incredulity as well as relief in his voice. 'That solves all your problems, doesn't it, Joanna?'

'What problems?' Catherine frowned.

Andrew hesitated, then ignoring Joanna's instinctive appeal, he turned to her mother. 'Shannon and Joanna are in love,' he told her quietly. 'They have been ever since Joanna went out to Kwyana.'

'What?' Catherine stared at her daughter. 'Is this true?'

'I—well, yes. I love Shannon,' replied Joanna quietly, ignoring his father's exasperated expression. 'Whether he loves me or not is another matter.'

'What are you talking about, Joanna?' Andrew was angry. 'You know he loves you.'

'Do I?' Joanna looked up at him steadily. Then she indicated the document in his hand. 'That proves that Shannon and I are not related, as you say. And Shannon must have seen that certificate, when he applied for his

175

passport.'

Andrew's lips worked soundlessly for a minute. Then he burst out: 'Well, what of it?'

'He must know that now Daddy's dead, it would be a simple matter to prove his identity,' she exclaimed.

'So?'

'He hasn't come, has he?'

Catherine was regarding them both as if they had gone slightly mad. 'You mean, Joanna—you mean that you and Shannon—want to get married?'

Joanna got up from her chair, moving restlessly about the room. 'I—I don't know. I—I thought we did——'

'*Joanna!*' Andrew's voice was hard and commanding. 'Stop pretending. You know you love Shannon. You know he loves you. You can't ignore what's between you.'

'Well, he has, hasn't he?' she cried piteously.

'You don't know that. Go to Kwyana and find out.'

'I—I can't.' She shook her head. 'Not now.'

'You must,' said Andrew with conviction. 'There's no other way.'

Joanna had wanted Andrew to come with her to Kwyana, but he had insisted on remaining at the hotel in Menawi.

'You must do this alone, Joanna,' he had told her firmly, and having come so far, she had no choice but to go on.

The halt at Kwyana was just as busy as on that other occasion when she had arrived here to see Shannon, and the heat was just as intense, overlaid with a humidity that was weakening in the early afternoon. Joanna had come up again in the train, not giving in to Andrew's suggestion to hire a car, mainly because her previous experience of car-riding in this country had not been memorable in any good sense of the word.

She was not really surprised to find the man Lorenz employed at his usual chore of loading and off-loading his lorry, but he was obviously surprised to see her.

'Well, well,' he exclaimed, when she had run the gamut of the crush on the concrete platform to reach him. 'It is Miss Carne, is it not? So Camilla decided to send for you, after all. She swore she would not do it, but she is sometimes foolish where your brother is concerned. Unfortunately, he does not seem to share her weakness.'

Joanna had listened to this confusedly, and now she exclaimed: 'What do you mean—send for me?'

Lorenz's eyes widened. 'You don't know!' he exclaimed, and then after assuring himself that she did not, he burst out laughing. 'Oh, but that is amusing!'

'What is amusing? Mr Lorenz, please—what are you talking about? Why should—why should Nurse Langley need to send for me? Is—is Shannon ill again?'

Lorenz sobered. 'You really don't know? No, I see you do not. Then I will tell you. Your brother had an accident, Miss Carne. Ten—eleven days ago. There was an explosion in the mine. Fourteen men were killed. Your brother was injured trying to get them out.'

'Oh, no!' Joanna felt sick. 'So where is he?'

'Where would he be but in the hospital at Kwyana? There are doctors there, good doctors. He is in good hands.'

'But how is he? How ill is he? What happened?'

Lorenz turned away to chivvy the African porters, and she had to contain her impatience until he was prepared to speak to her again.

'You want a ride to the mine?' he asked, turning back to her. 'Get in the lorry. I am nearly ready.'

'But Shannon ... How is he?' Joanna was desperate. 'Please—you must tell me. I must know.'

'Such concern for a brother!' Lorenz shook his head. 'Camilla does not show such concern for me.'

'Camilla is your sister?' Joanna stared at him. It explained so much, not least his attitude on her first journey to the mine.

'Yes, Camilla is my sister,' he agreed casually. 'You did

177

not know?'

Joanna shook her head, and he nodded.

'We are not so alike. She is intelligent, I am not. She is ambitious, I am lazy. She does not like you, Miss Carne.'

Joanna was almost in tears. 'Shannon,' she begged. 'How is Shannon?'

'He is not dying. He was lucky—he only got his ribs crushed and concussion. I think a rib punctured his lung, and this has caused some congestion, but he is recovering. He has been calling for you.'

'What?'

'Is true.' Lorenz nodded his head. 'Doctors say—who is this Joanna? Camilla—she say, I don't know.'

Joanna chewed hard on her lower lip. 'And it happened eleven days ago?'

'Ten, eleven days. I'm not sure.'

Joanna nodded. Andrew had been so right to make her come here. Ten days ago, her father had had his fatal attack.

She had been impatient on that last occasion to reach the mine, but nothing like as impatient as she was now. Rather than sit in the cab and wait for Lorenz, she wandered restlessly around outside until the heat and the flies and the smell of sweating bodies forced her to climb into the lorry.

The journey to the mine seemed endless. Her nerves were strung to fever pitch, and her heart was pounding like a drum. She wondered if Lorenz could hear it, but he just chewed away on an old cigar, humming tunelessly to himself as they negotiated the potholes in the road.

'You want to go to the hospital?' he inquired, when they finally began to descend down into the valley.

'Where else?' asked Joanna tautly, and he nodded.

'Camilla will not be pleased to see you, Miss Carne.'

'I'm sorry.'

Lorenz sighed. 'She knows, you know.'

'Knows? Knows what?'

178

'That Shannon Carne is not your brother, Miss Carne,' he answered laconically.

'What?' Joanna stared at him. 'But—but how?'

Lorenz shrugged. 'Your brother—ah, I'm sorry, but I still think of him that way—he was very bitter when he came to South Africa. He used to drink, too—quite a lot at first. When a man is—how do you say?—emotionally disturbed, he needs something. And he used to talk. Shannon Carne talked, Miss Carne. To my sister.'

Joanna nodded slowly. 'I see.' So that was why Camilla had not wanted her here. All the pieces in the jigsaw were steadily falling into place.

The hospital at Kwyana was clinically clean and very up-to-date, with all the latest technical equipment. It was stark and modern, and after Lorenz's truck, ascetically sanitary. A black nurse was seated behind the reception desk, and her surprise at seeing a strange white woman was ludicrous.

'You want something?' she asked, standing up, and Joanna nodded.

'I'm Joanna Carne,' she said, waiting for the words to sink in. 'I'd like to see—my brother.'

The nurse's dark eyes widened. 'You're—*Joanna*!' she exclaimed, and Joanna nodded. The nurse looked delighted, and a little of Joanna's apprehension left her. 'Mr Carne's been asking for you.'

Joanna drew a trembling breath. 'Can I see him?'

The nurse picked up a telephone. 'Just a minute, Miss Carne. I'll just check with Doctor Muhli, but I'm sure it will be all right.'

Joanna stiffened. 'Oh, please,' she began, before the nurse could dial a number. 'I've come all the way from England. Couldn't I—couldn't you just tell me which room is—is his? I'd—I'd like to surprise him.'

The nurse hesitated, but she replaced the receiver on its rest. 'Well,' she murmured. 'Mr Carne is much improved.

And Doctor Muhli was most concerned when no one could tell him who *Joanna* was.' She seemed to come to a decision. 'I'm sure he won't object, Miss Carne.' She came out from behind the desk and pointed along the corridor. 'Mr Carne's room is the one at the end. Number 23. You can't miss it.'

'Thank you.'

Joanna sped along the corridor on trembling legs. She was terrified lest Camilla should appear and prevent her from seeing Shannon, and this Doctor Muhli might well listen to her. But she reached her destination without incident, and peered breathlessly through the glass panel at the top of the door.

Her legs went weak when she saw Shannon. He was lying flat on his back, staring up at the ceiling, his brown chest half-concealed beneath the swathe of dressings. He looked so pale and thin, and before she could prevent herself, her fingers had closed on the handle and opened the door.

He looked towards the door as it opened, and then made an obviously painful effort to get up on his elbows when he saw who was standing there.

'Joanna?' he muttered disbelievingly. 'Dear God, is it really you?'

Joanna stepped right inside the room and closed the door, leaning back against it for a moment, too overcome with emotion to answer him. Shannon stared at her through narrowed eyes, and then he sank back against the pillows muttering: 'Oh, why did you have to come, Joanna, why did you have to come? Finding me like this. I'm too weak to send you away.'

His tortured words brought her up and away from the door, flying to the bed and kneeling down beside it, burying her face against his shoulder. 'Oh, Shannon!' she breathed, over and over again, 'we didn't know. We didn't know!'

She could feel him trembling and raised her head to look

180

into his face. Its gauntness tore her heart, even while the look in his eyes drove all other considerations from her head. With a whispered endearment, she put her mouth to his and was devastated by his urgent response. With a groan, he pulled her on to the bed beside him, and she was lying in his arms, returning his kisses with hungry satisfaction.

'Joanna, Joanna,' he breathed, into her neck, his hands parting her thin blouse, his mouth seeking the rounded softness beneath. 'Oh, God, I've wanted you, so much—so much . . .'

'Me, too,' she murmured, when she could get her breath, aware that he had kicked away the covers and she was lying close to his lean, hard body. 'Oh, Shannon, I was so afraid you'd turn me away.'

'Turn you away?' Her words made him lift his head and look down at her, and a sudden embarrassment brought the colour to her cheeks. 'What's wrong?' he asked, faint amusement in the possession in his eyes. 'Don't you want me to see how beautiful you are?'

She hid her face against his chest. 'When you didn't come home, I thought you'd changed your mind,' she whispered huskily.

'Changed my mind?' He was obviously confused. 'You—expected me to come back?'

Joanna ventured to look up at him. 'For—for the funeral,' she prompted softly, and was shocked by his astonishment. 'Don't you know that—that my father's dead?'

Shannon stared down at her through disbelieving eyes. 'No!' He blinked rapidly. 'No.' He seemed to be finding it hard to take in. 'Maxwell Carne is dead?'

Joanna nodded. 'Ten days ago.'

Shannon showed his comprehension. 'The explosion at the mine,' he muttered. 'I gather I was informed.'

'We sent a cable.'

'I didn't get it.' His lips tightened suddenly. 'I wonder

why.'

The same thought struck both of them, but Shannon put it into words, one word: 'Camilla!'

'You think—she kept it from you?' asked Joanna, frowning.

'I think it's likely.' Shannon was bitter. 'Oh, Joanna, since I came back, I've hardly seen Camilla. She knows how I feel about you. She knows you're not my sister.'

'Lorenz told me. He said she doesn't like me.'

Shannon gathered her closer. 'Camilla was never more than a friend, Joanna. But—do you realise what this means?'

'Do you?'

He nodded. 'It means I can find out how long it takes to disprove my identity.'

Joanna licked her lips. 'With—with that certificate, I should think it would take no time at all,' she ventured.

'What certificate?' Shannon looked puzzled.

'Your birth certificate.'

'My birth certificate?' Shannon shook his head. 'My darling, you're not making sense.'

'Shannon, your birth certificate shows your real father's name. Daddy only had your surname changed later.'

'What?' He lay back weakly against the pillows.

Joanna could see his complete bewilderment, and hope stirred in her heart. 'You must have seen your birth certificate, Shannon. You needed it to apply for your passport.'

'I suppose I did.' Shannon frowned, trying to think. Then he uttered an exclamation. 'No, I didn't see it,' he told her, frowning. 'I remember now. I asked your father for it when I was planning to leave for South Africa, and he said he'd get it out for me. Then I filled in all the forms, and he posted it for me. He must have put in the birth certificate himself. And I saw nothing odd in that. I never saw it at all. When the passport came back, it was opened along with the other mail, and by the time I got it, only the passport itself was in the envelope.'

'Oh, Shannon!' Joanna leant unthinkingly over him, drawing back aghast when she realised she was hurting him. She ran her fingers over the elastic bandage, and then bent her head to kiss it. 'I thought—I thought you had known and hadn't told me.'

'As if I would,' he muttered, winding a handful of her hair round his hand and bringing her head back to his. He looked at her disturbingly for several seconds, then his mouth curved sensuously as it sought hers. 'Hmm, Joanna, are you going to stay with me until I can make an honest woman of you?'

Joanna was submerged in a tide of feeling which threatened to overwhelm her, but suddenly she remembered that she had not come to Lushasa alone. With a supreme effort, she pushed him away from her, smiling at his pained expression.

'Darling, I have something else to tell you,' she whispered. 'Don't you want to know who your father really is?'

Shannon stretched back against the pillows. 'Some American airman. Your father told me that.'

'Did he?' Joanna bit her lip. 'Would you like to meet him?'

'To meet him?' Shannon stared at her uncomprehendingly. 'Now what are you saying?'

'Oh, Shannon, it's a long story, but briefly, your mother wrote to—to my father and told him she was going to tell this—this airman that he had a son.'

'Good God!'

'You can imagine how that affected Daddy. I think— I'm not sure, but I think that's what caused his stroke.'

Shannon shook his head. 'Poor Maxwell!'

Joanna's eyes widened. 'Do you feel sorry for him?'

'Of course I do. Any man so—concerned with pride, with possessions, was only to be pitied.'

Joanna paused for a moment and then went on: 'Anyway,

I think that's why Daddy decided you should have Mallowsdale. He was so afraid there'd be a scandal.'

'I know.'

'After—after you'd gone ...' The memory of the way of Shannon's departure was still to poignant for her to go on without a shudder of remembered despair, and guessing her feelings, Shannon drew her closer. Pressing her face against his warm body, she continued: 'After you'd gone, Matt managed beautifully, and I broke my engagement to Philip.' She felt his lips against her hair, and it was difficult to concentrate when all she wanted was for Shannon to make love to her. 'Then—then one evening, one terrible evening about ten days ago, this man arrived, this American. His name is Andrew Steinbeck. He's your father, Shannon.'

Shannon made a disbelieving sound. 'He came—to Mallowsdale?'

'Yes. He wanted to see you. Jacqueline—your mother, that is—didn't know you weren't to be found there.'

'Oh, God!'

'Daddy got very upset. That was what killed him.'

'Oh, my God!' Shannon shook his head. 'Poor old devil.'

Joanna sighed. 'If only he hadn't judged everyone by his standards. He was sure that Andrew was coming to England to claim you as his son. After all these years. When all he really wanted was to see you—a natural enough desire.'

'You said—Andrew—as if you know him well,' murmured Shannon, frowning.

Joanna half smiled. 'I feel as though I do. Oh, that may sound crazy to you, but he's—well, he's so like you. Just like you. Tall—only he's grey, instead of dark-haired, and so—handsome.'

Shannon buried his face in her neck. 'And where is this paragon of virtue now?'

'In Menawi.'

'What?'

'It's true. He—it was he who persuaded me to come here and see you for myself. Like I said, when you didn't respond to our cable, I thought—I thought ...'

'You're crazy, do you know that?' muttered Shannon, half angrily. 'Don't you know I love you more than—more than life itself?'

Joanna looked up at him wonderingly. Then she said quietly: 'He—Daddy, that is—he left you the estate.'

'Oh, God!' Shannon uttered a groan. 'Joanna, I don't want the estate.'

'I know that. But I had to tell you.'

'Does it make a difference?' he asked anxiously. 'I mean, you didn't just come here because of that, did you?'

'You know better than that.'

'I've got to be independent, you see. I can't take anything else from your father, do you understand?'

'I—I think so.'

Shannon sighed. 'My work is here, at Kwyana. It's not much of a place, I know, but in six months I'm to be moved to Menawi, and then it won't be so bad.'

Joanna looked at him with her heart in her eyes. 'Shannon, if I'm to live with you, it could be in Timbuktu for all I care!'

'And what about the estate?'

'I don't know. Since Daddy died, Mummy's coped wonderfully. She and Matthew work well together. You're instructed to look after her for her lifetime.'

'Am I?' Shannon frowned. 'Oh, Joanna, what problems your father created! What am I to do. I can't sell the estate. It's your mother's home.'

Joanna hesitated. Then she said: 'Let her run it. She and Matt. We can decide what to do with it later.'

'Like—keep it for our son?' suggested Shannon softly. 'That's not a bad idea. What was it your father used to say—there have always been Carnes at Mallowsdale?'

Joanna blushed again, and he bent to kiss her. But as his

185

body moved over hers, she protested: 'What about your father, Shannon? Would you mind if he came to Kwyana?' Shannon smoothed back the damp hair from her forehead. 'Do you want him to come?'

'Hmm,' she nodded.

'All right. But not today, and maybe not tomorrow. Right now, I just want you all to myself ...' and when the reception nurse tiptoed along the corridor some time later to make sure everything was all right, she stole back again with a mischievous smile of envy on her face.

Best Seller Romances

Romances you have loved

Mills & Boon Best Seller Romances are the love stories that have proved particularly popular with our readers. They really are "back by popular demand." These are the other titles to look out for this month.

THE DISTANT DREAM
by Lilian Peake

What a ridiculous situation to be in, thought Maretta – a bone of contention between Professor Harford Tudor and his son Rhian! At least it would have been ridiculous if it had not been so serious – fo she had fallen in love with one man, and didn't want to hurt the other What *should* she do?

THE MAN AT LA VALAISE
Mary Wibberley

Sacha Donnelly decided to holiday in Provence on her own and certainly didn't bargain on having to share her cottage with three strange men. How she longed to escape from Tor – the mysterious Nikolai Torlenkov – dark and disturbing, who had forced her to remain there. But soon Sacha was to wonder if she really wanted to get away . . .

Mills & Boon

DARLING INFIDEL
by Violet Winspear

Young Cathy Colt just couldn't stand the autocratic Dr. Woolf Maxwell, and she didn't care in the least when her glamorous friend Pippy announced that she was going to make him fall in love with her. But someone had warned Cathy, 'Beware of hate, it's first cousin to love.' Would she find out, too late, that that was perfectly true?

CHILD OF TAHITI
by Rebecca Caine

'You're too young to wear the flower of love,' Max Thornton told Tina, when she fled from Pierre and heartbreak. But three years later, when Pierre wanted her, she recognised the truth in her heart at last; it was Max she wanted all the time. But Max was no good, they told her...

ISLE OF THE GOLDEN DRUM
by Rebecca Stratton

Marys wasn't at all looking forward to being stranded for the next two months on a Pacific island with her tycoon boss and his son Michael, whom she had just refused to marry. But the two of them together were less of a problem than the island's owner, the inscrutable Griffort Campbell...

the rose of romance

ROMANCE

Variety is the spice of romance

Each month, Mills & Boon publish new romances. New stories about people falling in love. A world of variety in romance – from the best writers in the romantic world. Choose from these titles in October.

AN UNBROKEN MARRIAGE Penny Jordan
BETWEEN PRIDE AND PASSION Flora Kidd
A WILD AFFAIR Charlotte Lamb
RAPTURE OF THE DEEP Margaret Rome
MAKESHIFT MARRIAGE Marjorie Lewty
UNGUARDED MOMENT Sara Craven
THE MAN FROM NOWHERE Rebecca Stratton
BATTLE OF WILLS Victoria Gordon
GOLDEN FEVER Carole Mortimer
ALL OUR TOMORROWS Jan MacLean
DEVIL'S GOLD Nicola West
THE MAN FROM AMAZIBU BAY Yvonne Whittal

On sale where you buy paperbacks. If you require further information or have any difficulty obtaining them, write to: Mills & Boon Reader Service, PO Box 236, Thornton Road, Croydon, Surrey CR9 3RU, England.

Mills & Boon
the rose of romance